THE JUROR

Michael Underwood

ST. MARTIN'S PRESS
NEW YORK

Printed in Great Britain

First published in the United States of America in 1975
Library of Congress Catalog Card Number: 74-83585

To George Hardinge

CHAPTER ONE

'Looks a bit like the Moscow metro,' Vic Fielden had remarked knowingly to a group of fellow jurors in waiting that first morning ten days ago. 'Though not one of the better stations, mind you,' he had added with a salesman's embracing smile.

Later, it was this observation more than anything else which caused the others to elect Vic as their foreman, for anyone who could lightly compare the new wing of the Old Bailey with a station on Moscow's metro must have the qualities of leadership and *savoir-faire* desirable in a foreman of the jury. There may have been others present as well equipped, but their virtues had not been so readily on display and Vic Fielden was the last person to demur when three of his fellow jurors had proposed that he should assume the role.

That had been ten days ago. Ten days during which a wartime camaraderie had developed amongst them, fostered energetically by Vic himself, so that first names had been exchanged as the feeling of solidarity grew.

Not that everyone had fallen under the spell. Mr Brigstock and Mr White were two who had remained quietly aloof from the pervading spirit of togetherness and there were others who were not wholly committed. But at least half the jury could be classified as Vic's men; moreover, certain events since the trial began had brought additional converts. Anonymous threats to two of them had done much to bring them all closer together.

The trial for which Vic Fielden and eleven other males had been empanelled as jurors was in fact a re-trial after a jury disagreement at the first. The accused was Bernie Mostyn, a name unknown to the public at large, but not to the Metropolitan Police. A potent figure in the world of vice and pornography, Mostyn was charged with a whole range of offences arising out of his business activities, including intimidation, described in the indictment as an attempt to defeat the course of justice, and possessing quantities of pornographic material such as would make the British Museum look like a village library by comparison.

Mostyn's second trial was taking place before Judge Slingsby in a court on the third floor of the Old Bailey's new wing. Though the judge came fresh to the case, prosecuting and defending counsel were the same as on the first occasion.

The re-trial was being punctuated by an even greater number of legal submissions on behalf of the defence than the first. At the first breath of one of these, Judge Slingsby would send the jury scurrying to its room as though to save them from some deadly infection. He appeared to be in permanent fear that they might hear something which would require their discharge and the case to be started all over again.

It was these constant retirements, coupled with the fact that they had spent a whole eye-popping, mind-boggling day poring over samples of Bernie Mostyn's wares, that had given them unusual opportunities of becoming acquainted with one another.

Ever since he had been elected their foreman, it had become Vic Fielden's practice to arrive at court early and to await the others in the manner of a host looking out for guests.

On this particular morning, he was sitting on one of the back-to-back seats which run down the centre of the concourse outside the courts. Sitting immediately behind him were two barristers. Each time one of them leaned backwards, the queue of his wig tickled Vic's neck, which he found annoying, though the barrister seemed quite oblivious of the fact.

'Told my chap he'd get at least three years,' the barrister was saying in a loud voice, 'and then old Tankerton just gave him a long lecture with eighteen months suspended at the end. Enough to dent a client's faith in his counsel's judgment,' he added with a mirthless laugh.

His companion's only comment was a non-committal grunt.

At that moment, Vic observed two of his jurors approaching. He got up and waved to attract their attention.

' 'Morning, Jim, 'morning, Mr White. Everyone seems to be a bit late this morning.'

'Ian Berenger'll be here in a minute, he's just paying a call on his way up,' Jim Dunn said with a grin. 'Not sure I won't follow his example. Who was the sage who said something about never letting slip the golden opportunity of relieving nature?'

'Probably Napoleon,' Vic Fielden said with a happy chuckle. 'It sounds like Napoleon, don't you think, Mr White? Either him or Wellington.'

Robert White shook his head. 'I've no idea,' he said in a tone which caused the other two men to exchange resigned looks. He was older than both of them and lacked their trendy appearance. Indeed, if the defence hadn't run out of challenges, he would probably not have been on the jury at all as they had tended to challenge anyone who looked middle-aged and conservative as opposed to liberal and with-it. And yet, curiously, Robert White fitted none of these popular images. He was just himself.

Just then, Ian Berenger came up, accompanied by Mr Brigstock, another who had resisted Vic Fielden's blandishments.

'I wonder where Laurence is?' Fielden observed. 'He's usually one of the first here.'

'Which is Laurence?' Mr Brigstock asked.

'Mr Pewley.'

'Oh, him!'

The fact was that Mr Pewley gave Mr Brigstock the creeps and he was thankful he was not sitting next to him in the jury box. Mr Brigstock was not only sure he dyed his hair but there was something about his manner he found singularly distasteful. Moreover, he had been repelled by the lustful expressions that had flitted across Mr Pewley's face the day they had spent in the jury room pawing their way through all those books and magazines. It had been all too apparent that for him this was no obnoxious duty conscientiously performed. It was a positively enjoyable experience.

Mr Brigstock's determination not to succumb to what he regarded as Vic Fielden's saloon bar charm dated from that day. He still smarted when he recalled how their foreman had pretended to chide him in front of the others for confusing 'Whippers' with 'Whoppers' and how Mr Pewley had shoved a book across the table towards him with the insinuating comment, 'Here's one I bet you haven't got on your library list!' It had been *Suki and the Lash.*

'Should finish the prosecution case today,' Vic Fielden remarked with the air of an old hand.

'I was talking to one of the ushers and he says the defence are going to call dozens of witnesses,' Jim Dunn said.

'Dozens? Surely not,' Berenger replied. 'What on earth could they all say?'

Dunn shrugged. 'Search me! Almost everything that happens comes as a surprise to me!'

'Better keep your voices down,' Vic Fielden cautioned. 'Don't want anyone overhearing us.' He glanced quickly about him as if to catch some of Mostyn's witnesses in the act of eavesdropping. He turned back to his companions and did a rapid head count. 'Everyone's here now except Laurence. Wonder what's held him up?'

'Probably got stuck in the traffic,' someone remarked. 'Where does he have to come from?'

'He lives in Highbury,' Fielden said.

'He told me his was a pretty awful journey with changes of bus and underground,' a juror named Davey said.

'Perhaps he's been taken ill,' Berenger remarked.

'What happens then?' Jim Dunn asked.

'The trial goes on with eleven of us.' This contribution came from Mr White and they all turned in his direction.

'I'm not sure that's quite the position,' Vic Fielden said in what for him was a surprisingly tentative tone.

'I think you'll find it is,' Mr White replied. 'Anyway, I've certainly read in newspapers of cases going on with only eleven jurors. Sometimes, ten, I believe. Probably the judge decides.'

'I hope you're right,' Mr Brigstock said.

'Why?' Berenger asked in a puzzled tone.

'Why? Because of the waste of time and money if it's otherwise, of course.'

'Oh, I see! I was thinking we'd all get away a bit sooner.'

'What we ought to be hoping,' Vic Fielden said reprovingly, 'is that Laurence is only held up in the traffic.' He gave them all a meaningful look.

'You don't think something may have happened to him?' Dunn said anxiously.

'I hope not, but don't forget what happened to Philip and David.'

Philip Weir and David Davey had been the last two to arrive and everyone now glanced in their direction. They were much of an age, each being in his early thirties. Age apart, their only common characteristic was a certain weakness of feature. Weir was constantly moistening his lips and had a chin which looked perpetually on the verge of trembling and Davey's face was adorned by a not very satisfactory beard.

It had been on the third evening after the trial had begun that Weir, who lived with his parents, received a mysterious telephone call. The anonymous caller clearly knew he was a member of the Mostyn jury and had hinted at various disagreeable consequences if Mostyn were to be convicted. Philip Weir had decided that discretion was the better part of valour and would never have brought the matter to light but for what happened the next evening to David Davey.

A hundred yards short of his front gate in an ill-lit street in West Hampstead, Davey had been suddenly jostled off the pavement by somebody with the combined muscle of a rugby scrum who had then hurried off into the darkness, though not before he had passed a few audible comments on the hazards of jury work.

When Davey mentioned what had happened to Vic Fielden the next morning, Fielden said immediately they must tell the judge. He had then enquired whether anyone else had suffered a similar experience and Weir, emboldened by the solid atmosphere of the Old Bailey, told of his phone call.

Judge Slingsby failed to react with the display of judicial thunderbolts Vic Fielden and others had anticipated, though he did deliver a stern lecture on what he referred to as the heinous crime of embracery, which, they gathered, was the improbable name of the offence committed against the two jurors concerned. He had then said that any further attempts to interfere with the jury could have the most serious consequences, but he had circumspectly failed to specify what these might be. Finally he had glanced meaningfully at Detective Inspector Scriven, the officer in charge of the case.

Mr Gilbert Trapp Q.C., who was leading counsel for the defence, had risen to express his own indignation at what had befallen the two jurors and had assured the judge and everyone else in court that his client was certainly quite blameless in the matter. It was, he had said, the last thing that Mr Mostyn would indulge in and Bernie Mostyn had nodded energetically to emphasise the unthinkability of such conduct on his part.

'You think Laurence may have been beaten up or something?' Dunn said, breaking the silence.

Vic Fielden gave a portentous shrug.

'I suggest we don't indulge in idle speculation,' Mr Brigstock remarked.

'And I second that,' Mr White added, before anyone else could speak.

Vic Fielden pursed his lips. 'I'm sorry you think it's only idle speculation,' he said, stiffly. Then: 'It's time for us to go into court. I see the usher signalling us.'

'A little authority goes to some people's heads like a whiff of gas,' Mr Brigstock observed to Mr White as they all trooped towards the entrance.

After they had taken their places in the jury box, Vic Fielden whispered to an usher whose eyes moved along the front row to the gap at the further end between Mr White and David Davey. The usher nodded and went over to speak to the clerk of the court who had just entered.

The clerk gave a brief nod and, turning in the jury's direction, read out their names as he did each morning before the judge took his seat. Their responses to the roll call were no longer the nervous acknowledgements of presence they had been on the first couple of mornings, but were now a mixture of the confident and the blasé.

'Laurence Pewley,' the clerk called out, but paused only a second before going on to the next name.

Knocks on the judge's door indicated his imminent arrival in court and Vic Fielden cast a quick proprietorial glance round his band of ten before giving Judge Slingsby the sort of bow appropriate to an eastern potentate.

The judge sat down and the clerk turned round to have a short whispered conversation with him. When the clerk resumed his seat, Judge Slingsby addressed prosecuting and defending counsel who sat facing him.

'Mr Culshaw, Mr Trapp, the court has received a telephone message indicating that a member of the jury has been taken ill and is unlikely to be fit enough to return for several days. In these circumstances, I have had to decide whether to continue the trial with eleven jurors or whether to discharge this jury and order a re-trial. As you will know, since the Criminal Justice Act of 1965, it is a matter entirely for my discretion and I have reached the decision that the interests of justice will be best served if the case goes on.' He gave counsel a small, wintry smile. 'May I take it that neither of you wish to say anything to cause me to review the decision I have reached?'

Robin Culshaw, one of the senior Treasury Counsel at the Old Bailey, got up and said that the crown was more than anxious not to have the trial aborted and Gilbert Trapp, using rather more words, said the same thing.

Judge Slingsby looked over their heads at Mostyn sitting in the dock behind counsel's seats. The defendant's face was a mask of impassivity.

What the judge had not mentioned in open court was that, in the light of earlier events, he had deemed it prudent to ask for discreet enquiries to be made as to the precise nature of Mr Pewley's illness.

It was during the lunch adjournment he was informed that the absent juror was not at his home and that his flat was locked and appeared deserted, with curtains still drawn across the windows in the middle of the morning.

CHAPTER TWO

Jessamyn Park in North London was not much of a park; indeed, many would have regarded it as hardly worthy of the name, it being less than three acres in size. But for one person it was a small cherished world.

For a quarter of a century it had been looked after by Fred Huggins, who planted its flower beds, mowed its grass, swept up its leaves, bellowed at its destructive children and hounded courting couples out of its bushes. The seasons might change and bring fresh patterns to Fred's work, but he himself seemed never to change, other than to put on a donkey jacket when November came and take it off in April. He was a small, wiry man with sharp features and a pair of darting, suspicious eyes. He seldom spoke to anyone and users of the park who addressed him were generally favoured by no more than a grunted monosyllable.

The park was traversed by two asphalt footpaths, each of which provided a short cut for pedestrians, most of whom scarcely noticed their surroundings as they hurried to and fro. Such people earned Fred's strongest contempt, even though they gave him no trouble. To walk through Jessamyn Park oblivious of its charms just about summed up man's lost sense of values in his view.

But if there was one season of the year that habitually brought Fred Huggins to the state of an animal at bay it was late autumn when the park was covered with fallen leaves which the wind scattered as soon as he had gathered them up. And if not the wind, then children, who delighted in romping in the mountainous piles as soon as his back was turned. And when by chance the leaves were too wet to be blown by the wind or sent flying by the children, there were complaints to the local town hall about the danger to old people slipping on them. This inevitably brought along the superintendent of parks, a man for whom Fred Huggins reserved his deepest contempt of all, regarding him as a petty bureaucrat, who cared nothing for parks and plainly resented leaving his warm office to come and speak to Fred. Happily, their meetings were always short, with maximum frustration apparent on both sides.

Fred was still seething over a visit from the superintendent that morning when he decided to knock off a bit early. It had been an overcast day and by four o'clock the gloom of a November afternoon discouraged any further endeavour.

With some relish, he tamped down the leaves in his hand-cart to prevent those on top falling off and made his way to the master pile behind his hut over in one corner of the park. Once a week one of the council's lorries came and collected them from there.

When he reached the pile, he tilted his cart to empty it and then fetched his long broom to sweep everything tidy round the base of the pile. It was while he was doing this that his broom struck against something unyielding just below the surface of the leaves. He paused a second, then went through the same motion again only to meet the same resistance.

'What's some bugger been playing at?' Fred muttered crossly and bent down to explore with his hands what alien object had found its way into his pile of leaves. A second later he leapt back with a strangulated oath. 'What the bugger!'

He stared at the place with a mixture of anger and alarm, as his brain told him quite clearly that what he had touched was a nose on a human face.

Bending down again, he gingerly brushed away the leaves until the grisly object was exposed. Then fetching his large hand-lamp from the hut, he turned its powerful beam on to the scene.

Beneath his gaze lay the head of a dead man. A head, moreover, as hairless as a billiard ball.

As an old soldier who had seen a fair amount of active service, Fred had learnt to accept the sight of dead men without qualm, but there was something particularly blood-chilling about the corpse that lay half covered in leaves at his feet.

It was the completely hairless head which held him rooted to the spot as though hypnotised. Eventually, however, he tore his gaze away and, picking up a piece of sacking, threw it over the body. Then muttering furiously to himself, he hurried to the telephone kiosk which lay just beyond the park bounds and called the police.

CHAPTER THREE

Detective Sergeant Nick Attwell was grateful for the piece of luck which caused him to be the first C.I.D. officer on the scene. He was a keen young officer, still in his twenties, who had joined the Metropolitan Police for all the right reasons. That is to say, he had responded to the recruiting advertisements extolling the job as a thoroughly worthwhile one to all young men with a spirit of service and adventure. He had been marked out for early promotion and transferred from the uniform branch to the C.I.D. He was never happier than when he was busy, and, for him, 'being busy' didn't mean sitting in an office writing reports, but being out and about investigating crimes.

He had happened to be in a radio patrol car in the

vicinity of Jessamyn Park when the call went out so that he and his crew arrived within three or four minutes of Fred Huggins leaving the telephone kiosk.

Leaving the driver in the car, Sergeant Attwell and a uniformed constable dashed into the park and ran over to Fred's hut where they could see a light in a window.

'You the police?' Fred asked, peering at them in the darkness. 'You got here quick.'

'I take it you're the park-keeper who made the call?' Nick said.

'Fair bugger it is! Didn't 'arf give me a start.'

'The body you mean?'

'Don't know what some bugger's being playing at! How'd it get there, that's what I'd like to know?'

'Whereabouts is the body?'

'Yonder under them leaves. I covered him over with a bit of sacking, respectful like.'

When they reached the place, Nick bent down and lifted the piece of sacking. 'Give us your lamp a moment,' he said.

For several seconds they stood silently staring at as much of the corpse as was revealed while Fred Huggins fidgeted beside them still muttering at what he obviously regarded as a personal affront.

'Ever seen the dead man before?' Nick enquired, shining the lamp on Fred.

'Not likely!'

'What I meant was, he's not someone who frequents the park?'

'Couldn't forget his 'ead, could I? Only ever seen his likes once before. When I was in army. Chap called Curly Jones. 'E 'ad an 'ead like that. 'S'why 'e was called Curly.'

'This chap may have worn a wig.'

'Where is it then?'

'We'll make a thorough search as soon as we can.'

'Why not now?'

'Can't disturb the body until the doctor's been. We'll also want to take some photographs before anything's moved.' He turned to the uniformed P.C. 'Get back to the car, Bob, and let headquarters know. Then stop anyone approaching this part of the park. I'll be in the hut seeing if I can find out a bit more from our friend here.'

When they were inside the hut, Fred made to close the door, but Nick stopped him.

'Better leave it open so as I can keep an eye on things outside.'

'Bit cold ain't it?'

''Fraid we'll have to put up with that.'

Fred gave a disgusted snort and, reaching into an ancient haversack on the floor, fetched out a billycan.

'Like a drop?' he asked.

'Tea, is it?'

''Course it's tea!'

'Thanks. Not often you see those things these days,' Nick said, nodding at the billycan.

'Better'n all your new fangled thermy flasks.'

'Tea's good.'

''Course it's good! Made it meself.'

Nick waited until Fred had finished rolling a cigarette before going on.

'Have you any idea when the body could have got there?'

'Not while I've been 'ere today, it couldn't.'

'Do many people cross the park at night?'

'They comes and goes.'

'But I imagine there must be longish periods when the park's empty.'

'Apart from them in the bushes.'

'Courting couples?'

'And nancy boys.'

'Even on a cold November night?'

'They don't stop long. Just 'ave their so-called fun and off.'

'I hadn't heard that Jessamyn Park was troubled in that way. However, the point is that somebody could probably dump a body here at night without being spotted.'

'They couldn't while I'm 'ere, that's for sure.'

'Are you able to say that the body wasn't there yesterday?'

'Couldn't 'ave been. That pile of leaves was what I collected yesterday. The lorry came yesterday morning and took the last lot away.'

'So it must have been last night that the body was put there?'

'Seems that way.'

'Well, that's a start. It's when you don't know how long dead bodies have been around that you're faced with difficulties.'

Fred shook his head in a bemused fashion.

'Fancy some bugger 'iding a body in my leaves! And 'im with no 'air either.'

'That should also make him easier to identify.'

''Ow d'you think 'e died?'

'Looked to me as though he had marks on his throat, so my guess is he was strangled.' Nick stepped over to the door and looked out. 'I think someone's coming. It'll probably be the doctor.'

Dr Parsons was the divisional surgeon. His principal role for the police was to turn out at all hours to take blood samples from drunken drivers, certify prisoners as fit to be detained in the police cells and to treat those suffering from minor injuries. In addition, he was often called to examine manifestly dead bodies before they were removed to the mortuary or, as now, before one of the forensic pathologists could get to the scene and conduct a preliminary examination. It was an aspect of his work which he regarded as a complete waste of time.

'Well, where's this body?' he asked briskly, as Nick stepped out of the hut on his approach.

'Just over here, sir.'

When they arrived at the place, Nick shone the lamp on to the corpse and Dr Parsons squatted down beside it. A couple of minutes later he straightened up.

'He's dead. Very dead,' he said solemnly.

'So I surmised, sir.'

'But call a doctor in to make sure ... All right, all right, that's not fair of me. I know it's not your fault.'

'Can you say how long he's been dead, sir?'

'A goodly time.'

'It seems he may have been killed some time last night and dumped here.'

'That would figure. Can't make any accurate guesses just by looking at him and touching his skin, but he's certainly been dead a fair number of hours. Any idea who he is?'

'None.'

'You shouldn't have too much difficulty identifying him with that head. Makes one grateful for one's own hair. The cranium is best covered up.' He paused. 'The human body is a good piece of practical construction, but there's nothing very elegant about it.' He gave Nick a penetrating glance. 'Compare any Miss World with a thoroughbred horse; the one's as ungainly as the other is streamlined.'

'I'd still sooner ...'

'Of course you would at your age,' Dr Parsons said without waiting for the sentence to be completed. 'Incidentally, for what it's worth, it looks as though he was garrotted. Strangled from behind. Well, if that's all, I'll be getting back. I was just putting my feet up for the first time today when your lot called me out.'

'Thanks for coming, sir.'

'I won't say it's been a pleasure, because it hasn't. But that's not your fault.' As they turned away from the scene, he asked, 'Who discovered the body?'

'The park-keeper.'

'Old Fred Huggins?'

'Yes. He's in the hut now.'

'He's a patient of mine. He won't have approved of people leaving corpses in his park.'

'He doesn't.'

As they reached the hut, Dr Parsons stuck his head through the door. ''Evening, Mr Huggins.'

''Evening, doctor. Like a cup of tea?'

'Thank you, no. I'm going home to something more medicinal than tea.'

'I could do with a drop of the 'ard stuff myself.'

'I'm sure you could,' Dr Parsons said in a solicitous tone. 'It must have been a nasty shock, finding that body.'

'It was 'im 'aving no 'air. Don't want to say nothink against the dead, but 'e'd give anyone the shivers.'

Dr Parsons nodded sympathetically. He turned to Nick who was hovering a yard away. 'Can't you let him go home?'

'I'd just like him to wait until my guvnor comes, sir. He should be here quite soon, I gather, and then he'll take charge of the investigation.'

'Haven't seen him for several weeks, how is he?'

'He's all right, sir. He only got back from leave a couple of days ago.'

'Lucky fellow!'

Nick refrained from pointing out that Detective Chief Superintendent Peacock had twice had to postpone his leave during the summer months and had finally spent ten November days in Tunisia where it rained for most of the time and he was laid low with a tummy upset.

With the departure of the doctor, Nick returned to the hut. He hadn't been there long, however, before Detective Chief Superintendent Peacock, Professor Trimmer, the pathologist, and one of the civilian photographers from the photographic section at Scotland Yard arrived in quick succession.

By this time, too, news had spread and the police were moving people on whenever they approached the area which had been roped off.

Professor Trimmer waited for the photographer to complete his work before starting on his own examination of the scene. This done, he stood up, brushed himself down and turning to Peacock said, 'See you at the mortuary.'

The body was lifted on to a stretcher, covered with a blanket and carried out of the park to a waiting ambulance, where a couple of dozen people craned forward for a glimpse of the unrevealing spectacle.

'I want you to stay here, Nick, and comb through that pile of leaves,' Chief Superintendent Peacock said. 'I'll send D.C.s Bateman and Cash to help you. I'll also try and organise some light for you.' He glanced about him with a doubtful expression. 'Not much chance of finding any footprints that'll help.'

'I've already had a look, sir, and there doesn't appear to be anything. Normally, only the park-keeper would have any reason to come into this particular corner, but there's nothing to stop anyone else following the path round to the hut.'

Peacock nodded. 'I doubt, too, whether you'll find anything in that pile of leaves, but we've got to check. There's just a possibility that if he was wearing a wig, or even a hat, it's buried in there somewhere.'

'People in that sort of hairless condition usually wear one or the other, sir.'

'I'm damned sure I should.'

It was not long after Chief Superintendent Peacock's departure that a specially equipped police vehicle arrived and three powerful lamps were positioned round the area. A generator was started up and suddenly the scene outside Fred's hut was as brilliantly lit as a film-set. Fred himself had meanwhile gone home on the understanding that he would stay in and be available for further questions should the police wish to see him again that evening.

For forty minutes, Nick and his companions scoured the area, but without finding anything of significance. When they came to examine their pickings, it was to find that they consisted of sodden cigarette packets, chocolate wrappings and a couple of battered Coca-Cola tins. Indeed, the only item worth removal in Nick's view was the sample of leaves taken from where the corpse had lain.

If the dead man had been wearing anything at all on his head, it had vanished. The inference seemed to be that he hadn't.

Leaving the area guarded by two uniformed P.C.s, the three C.I.D. officers departed, Nick and Cash for the mortuary and Bateman to return to the Station.

When they reached the mortuary, Professor Trimmer was part-way through his examination. Lying unclothed on the marble slab, the dead man appeared to have shrunk. His smooth, bald pate gleamed beneath the light like the surface of a freshly opened tin of wax polish.

Detective Chief Superintendent Peacock was sitting by himself over in a corner of the mortuary. He had seen more post mortem examinations in his career than he had had hot dinners and he no longer felt either the desire or the need to hang over the body while it was being treated with the absence of dignity that corpses receive. Peacock, a reflective and, indeed, basically religious man, invariably pondered this whenever he was in a mortuary. He presumed that the dignity of man lay entirely in his spirit and that, without his spirit, one shouldn't expect to find any dignity left.

He motioned to Nick to sit down beside him.

'Find anything?'

'Nothing, sir.'

'Not a single identifying mark on any of his clothing either. And what's more remarkable, no personal possessions at all. No wallet, no driving licence, no cigarette case. Only some keys.'

'It looks as if the murderer may have removed them to prevent identification.'

'There is another possibility.'

'What's that, sir?'

'He left all identifying items at home because he was out on the prowl.'

'After sex, you mean?'

'Could be.'

'Boys?'

'Could be.'

'Has Professor Trimmer given the cause of death yet?'

'He was strangled from behind. Something was slipped over his head and twisted very quickly and very tightly round his neck. He didn't have time to put up any struggle.'

'Any clue as to what was used?'

'The professor thinks it was a piece of cord. He's taking away pieces of neck tissue for microscopic examination.'

'What age does he think the chap was, sir?'

'What's your guess?'

'Around forty.'

'Not bad. The professor says early forties. Also that he was suffering from *alopecia areata*.'

'What on earth's that?'

'That's his baldness. Normally, it's temporary following an illness, but this bloke's hair never grew again and the condition was permanent.'

They looked across to where Professor Trimmer was bent over the body. His secretary sat on a hard chair close by, her shorthand notebook open, her pencil poised. D.C. Cash was busily engaged placing the dead man's clothing into plastic bags and labelling them.

'Unless he was killed elsewhere and brought to Jessamyn Park and dumped there,' Peacock said, thoughtfully, 'the odds are he lives in the locality. And if he lives in the locality, the odds are that he lives alone, seeing that we haven't received any reports of anyone missing from their home.'

Nick nodded. 'It seems to me highly unlikely, sir, that he was murdered elsewhere and that his body was brought to the park. If you were going to that sort of trouble, there are far better places to deposit bodies than Jessamyn Park.'

'That's a point. We'd better have door to door enquiries made, starting with the houses in the roads leading to the park. I want to know whether anyone heard or saw anything suspicious last night.'

'Professor Trimmer thinks that was when he was killed does he, sir?'

'Yes. Says he's been dead between eighteen and twenty-four hours.'

'That means between about seven last night and three o'clock this morning.'

'That's about it. I don't remember, what's the lighting in the park?'

'There's a lamp at each of the four entrances and one in the middle where the paths intersect, except that's not been working for several days.'

'So the middle of the park would be pretty dark?'

'More than just the middle, sir. None of the lamps casts much of a light.'

Although Jessamyn Park fell within Detective Chief Superintendent Peacock's divisional area, it was only just so and the boundary lay a hundred yards on its west side. It was this which prompted Peacock to say, 'We must liaise with our neighbours as soon as we get back to the Station.'

As things turned out, however, the initiative came from the other side. There was a message from Detective Chief Inspector Frant, the acting head of the C.I.D. in the neighbouring division, saying that he understood a murder had been committed on Mr Peacock's patch and would he please phone him at his earliest convenience.

'Why didn't someone let me know at the mortuary?' Peacock asked, crossly.

'You'd already left, sir,' said temporary Detective Constable Irwin with an uncomfortable squirm. As the junior member of the C.I.D. he felt he was always being got at. The truth was that, though conscientious, he was not a very effective officer.

'Oh! Well, get Mr Frant for me now.'

A moment later, the call was put through.

'Thought I'd better have a word with you, sir,' Frant said. 'I gather you're having difficulty identifying the body found in Jessamyn Park. I just wondered whether there was any connection between your murder and a chap missing on this division. A man named Pewley who's a member of an Old Bailey jury and who failed to turn up this morning. I was asked to make discreet enquiries at his home as it was reported he was ill. But as far as I could see, he wasn't there and the place was deserted.'

'Is he someone with a completely bald head?'

'Not as far as I know. But I wasn't given a description. I was simply asked to find out what was wrong with him.'

'And?'

'I made my report and that's the last I heard. It's only hearing of your murder that's made me wonder ...'

'It makes me wonder, too. Where did this Pewley live?'

'Twelve High Tree Close. It's less than a mile from Jessamyn Park.'

'Can we go along there now?'

'Sure. Will you come and pick me up?'

'I'm on my way. Come on, Nick. It may be a fool's errand.' He paused. 'On the other hand, I have a feeling it may not be.'

CHAPTER FOUR

Whoever had given the name High Tree Close to the V-shaped road in which number 12 stood at the apex had obviously been more moved by imagination than any feeling for accurate description.

The houses on either side had seen better days and were, for the most part, a mixture of Victorian villas with an occasional modern duplex squashed in between to indicate that someone must have wrenched development permission from the local council and built for a quick profit.

It was the sort of road commonly found in London of the mid-seventies, which belonged to no one class or income group; though it was hardly the haunt of millionaires.

Where the two arms of the V met was a pair of high gates, with a '12' boldly painted on the left-hand one. Only the roof of the building beyond could be seen owing to their height and to the fact that the ground sloped away on the farther side.

'It's an old coach house,' Frant said, as he pushed open the right-hand gate. 'The ground level area is used as a store-room by a second-hand furniture dealer who rents it separately. This Pewley fellow lives above and has access to his place up that staircase.' He pointed to an unprotected iron stairway which ran up one end of the building.

They were standing in a paved yard which would hold a small car but nothing larger.

'What happens on the other side?' Peacock asked as they walked towards the stairway.

'A couple of laurel bushes, a lot of rubbish and a

high wall. There's a small park on the far side of the wall and one has the impression that people throw their litter into number twelve rather than leave it in the park.'

'Very public-spirited of them, I'm sure,' Peacock murmured.

'Obviously, it didn't bother Mr Pewley. Perhaps because, as far as I can see, the only room that looks out on that side is the bathroom. And *its* window is frosted glass.'

When they reached the door at the top of the stairs, Frant put his finger on the bell-push and held it there for several seconds. They could hear the bell ringing inside, but there was no sound of movement.

'O.K., let's try those keys you brought along,' Peacock said. 'And if none of them work, get ready to use your shoulder, Nick.' While Detective Chief Inspector Frant inserted the first key of his highly professional looking bunch, Peacock gazed out over the top of the double gate at the two arms of the road. 'Every coming and going of Mr Pewley and his friends must be visible for a hundred yards up either stretch.'

'The odds are we've been spotted and someone's phoning the police at this very moment about three suspicious figures trying to force an entry.'

Detective Chief Superintendent Peacock grunted. Laying oneself open to civil claims, if not criminal charges, was an occupational hazard which he and his ilk accepted. You broke down someone's door because you thought they were dying inside and then they suddenly came up very much alive behind you and raised hell, wanting to see you sued and prosecuted in every court of the land. Well, it was all part of the job.

'Can't you open it?' he asked, a trifle impatiently.

'This key almost seems to do the trick, but not quite.'

'Let Sergeant Attwell have a try!'

Nick replaced Frant at the door and began fiddling with the key, turning it this way and that.

'I don't want it to snap off in the lock,' he said, extracting it and bending down to peer through the keyhole.

'If three police officers are beaten by a lousy front door, things have reached a pretty pass,' Peacock remarked.

'It's all right, sir, I think this one'll do it. Yes, it's going to open.'

A second or two later they stepped into a narrow passage. Nick switched on a light and, without further word, each made for a different room.

'Well, there's no one here,' Peacock said, emerging from the living-room.

'Nor in the bedroom,' Frant called out.

Nick who had been examining the kitchen and bathroom joined the other two back in the passage. He shook his head in reply to Peacock's questioning look.

'Everywhere ship-shape, too,' Peacock said. 'No sign at all of disorder. Indeed, I'd say that Mr Pewley is a very tidy person. Or was!'

'Not only makes his bed, but puts a quilt on it,' Frant observed.

'Let's start in there,' Peacock said. 'One often learns more from a bedroom than elsewhere.' He stepped through the door, followed by the other two. 'One single divan bed, one built-in cupboard and one mahogany chest of drawers,' he murmured, looking about him. 'And under foot, one purple fitted carpet.'

He motioned to Nick to open the cupboard, which had sliding-doors. Hanging inside was a dark suit of conventional cut and beside it another which could have been bought in Carnaby Street. There were also three pairs of slacks, one made of faded blue denim, another cherry-coloured and the third being of black velvet. Beneath the clothes on the floor of the cupboard was a neat row of shoes, which, like the clothing, ranged from the conventional to the temporarily fashionable.

'Obviously, quite a snazzy dresser when he wanted to

be,' Peacock said. 'What's on the shelf above?'

The shelf at the top of the cupboard was curtained off by a piece of dark green material which Nick now pulled aside. There in a row, each on its own mushroom-shaped stand, were four wigs. It wasn't so much the number as the fact that each was different which caused the three beholders to stare in silence for several seconds.

'Quite a little display!' Peacock remarked, still gazing at the shelf. 'And it seems to settle one matter beyond much dispute, namely that our dead body and the missing Mr Pewley are one and the same person.'

'I wonder what happened to the wig he was wearing when he was murdered?' Nick Attwell said.

'If he was wearing one.'

'Wouldn't have thought, sir, he was the sort of person to go out without one.'

'Probably not.'

'It may have fallen off in the struggle,' Frant said.

'Fetch them down, Nick. We'll want to take possession of them, anyway.'

Nick reached up for the one nearest to him. It was a mousey-coloured, urchin cut hair piece which would fit close to the head. Next to it was a much more luxurious one, chestnut in colour and with a suggestion of curliness at the back. The third was a rich growth of iron grey hair which called for a pair of heavy horn-rimmed spectacles to go with it. The final one had a more workaday appearance and, when examined, also looked the most worn.

'Something for every occasion,' Peacock said, gingerly putting the chestnut coloured one back on its stand. 'Which do you think he wore for jury service?'

'I'd say the grey one, but I'm probably wrong,' Frant replied. 'But that's something we can find out quite easily.'

Peacock nodded and glanced at his watch. Then turning to Detective Chief Inspector Frant, he asked, 'Do you happen to know the name of the officer in charge of the case on which Pewley was a juror?'

'Detective Chief Inspector Scriven of the vice squad at the Yard.'

'See if you can run him to earth on the phone, Nick, and get a description of Pewley from him. Better than that, he'd better come out to the mortuary. Use the phone in the next room.' He turned back to Frant. 'Let's complete our search here.'

But nothing further of any interest came to light and they were about to leave the bedroom when Nick appeared in the doorway.

'I managed to speak to Mr Scriven, sir, and he's coming out immediately. He says the missing juror, as he recalls him, had fairly long brown hair.'

'That makes it the chestnut wig,' Peacock observed. 'Obviously jury service called for trendiness.' He moved towards the door. 'We'll now take a look round the living-room.'

Frant and Nick followed him into the room next door which was not much larger than the bedroom and had a crammed appearance, largely due to an enormous square black cushion which filled the centre of the room and which, Nick reckoned, would seat eight people, two on each of its sides.

'What on earth's that thing for?' Peacock asked, staring at it incredulously.

'Sitting on, sir.'

'Sitting on? But there's nothing to lean against.'

'They're in fashion nowadays.'

'To me, it looks both uncomfortable and immoral. It's an invitation to fireside sex.'

Nick, who had recently become engaged, refrained from asking what was wrong with that.

Peacock's gaze lifted from this object of suspicion and turned to a bookcase against the farther wall. At least, one end was a bookcase with sliding glass doors and the other consisted of three drawers. He walked across to it and, after a cursory glance at the books, all paperbacks, he opened the top drawer. Nick, who had followed him over, saw that it contained business papers neatly assembled in bulldog clips.

'Orderly to the point of fussiness, I'd say,' Peacock remarked, closing the drawer again.

He tried the next one down but found it locked, as was the bottom one.

'Wonder what's in those two?'

'I've brought his keys with me, sir,' Nick said, helpfully.

Peacock's head shot round as though his sergeant had blasphemed. 'Then what the blazes was all that fight for to open the front door?'

'There are no door keys on this ring, sir. You can see they're just small keys.'

'He must have had a door key on him,' Peacock said, accusingly.

'I'll check again when we get back, sir, but I don't remember seeing one.'

'O.K. Meanwhile let's see if any of those open either of these drawers.'

Nick selected a key and tried it. Peacock gave a satisfied grunt as it turned in the lock and Nick pulled the drawer open.

'Well, well, what have we here!'

'Looks like a stock of porn, sir.' And porn it was, though of a mild variety. There were several numbers of a nature magazine, containing photographs of insipid young men posing beside pieces of garden statuary or gazing mystically into the distance. There were also a large number of so-called health magazines in which males wearing boxing shorts contorted their torsos to reveal bizarre muscle development.

'Don't know why he wants to keep these locked up,' Peacock grumbled.

'I suppose they tell one something about his character, sir. Something he preferred to keep hidden.'

"All they tell me is that he had more money than sense. Fancy buying that sort of rubbish.'

'Chacun à son goût,' Nick murmured.

'I don't know what it means, but it sounds dirty. Moreover, what the hell's the force coming to when detective sergeants spout French at you on a murder enquiry!' He gave Nick a sardonic look. 'I suppose it was French?'

'Yes, sir. It means ...'

'Never mind what it means, open that bottom drawer.'

'Yes, sir.'

As Nick knelt down to do so, Peacock raised his eyebrows in mock despair and gave Frant a small grin. The grin turned into a frown as the drawer was pulled open to reveal a number of bulging loose-leaf notebooks.

'Look like press cuttings, sir,' Nick said as he lifted out three of the notebooks. He handed one each to Peacock and Frant and began thumbing through the third one himself.

'Ex Mayor on sex charge,' ran the headline of the first cutting his eyes fell upon. On the next page was one which read, 'Police Search for Missing Bank Clerk'. On the next, 'Well Known Author Accused by Au Pair Girl'. He turned another page. 'Peer Denies Choirboy's Allegations', sprang at him in bold capitals.

Each cutting was carefully pasted on to a page and neatly folded to preserve it intact.

A glance at the other two men told him that their books contained similar cuttings. He turned his attention back to the drawer and saw that there were seven more notebooks, making ten in all. At the back of the drawer was a small card index box which he reached for. It was full of cards in apparent alphabetical order and he extracted one at random.

'BAKER, Gordon Arthur' it read at the top left-hand corner. Beneath the name was written 'absconding cashier of Bristol company' and to the right of that piece of information was a reference to three newspaper reports, two dated 22nd May five years previously and one dated only a few months ago. In the bottom right-hand corner was a reference to the notebooks in which the press cuttings about Mr Baker had presumably been filed.

Nick selected another card. This one related to 'LING, Joseph Maxted', described beneath as 'blackmailer'. In his case there was only one newspaper reference. To an evening paper dated October the previous year.

He pulled out all the cards under 'S'. SANDS, SELLING, SITCH, SOMERS, SOWERBY, SUTTER and SWEET. They were variously described as 'wanted on sex charge', 'wealthy co-respondent', 'Soho Club Manager', adulterer', 'fancier of little girls', 'tax fiddler' and 'vanished treasurer'.

He turned back to the card relating to SWEET, Carlo, Soho club manager, and saw that there was a reference on it to 8/45. This he took to mean page 45 of notebook number 8. On putting this assumption to the test, he found it to be correct. There were no fewer than four cuttings relating to Carlo Sweet who was described as assisting the police in their enquiries into a beating-up which had taken place in Mr Sweet's club. A later cutting indicated that no charges had been preferred and there was a photograph of a smiling Carlo Sweet who professed himself ready at all times to assist the police in their difficult job and regretful that he'd been unable to give them any useful information on this occasion.

The silence which had fallen was now broken by Detective Chief Superintendent Peacock. 'Assuming this was a hobby, it was a very curious one.'

'It isn't just the cuttings, sir,' Nick said, holding up the box of cards. 'It's the fact that he referenced them all.'

Peacock took the cards from him and flicked through half a dozen. When he handed the box back, he said, 'The wonder is that no one had murdered him before.'

'He certainly appears to be a type-cast victim,' Nick observed.

'We'll take all that lot away with us. Get the wigs, too, Nick; and make sure the place is secure. We've enough to be getting on with, but we may want to have a further search later on.'

After dropping Frant at his Station, they drove to the mortuary where they arrived at almost the same moment as Detective Chief Inspector Scriven.

The mortuary attendant pulled out the refrigerated drawer in which Mr Pewley's hairless body lay cold and cobbled.

Scriven stared at it as though he were trying to get meaning from a piece of abstract sculpture.

'Prop him up, Nick,' Peacock said.

With an expression of distaste, Nick placed his hands beneath the dead man's shoulders and levered him into a sitting position. As he did so, Peacock placed the chestnut coloured wig on to the head.

'Is he more recognisable now?' Scriven nodded. 'Yes, that's him all right. Surprising what a difference the hair makes.'

'You're sure?'

'Certain.'

During the next quarter of an hour, Peacock told Scriven of the finding of the body and of the search of Mr Pewley's flat, and Scriven, in turn, gave a resumé of the Mostyn case and mentioned the threats which had been made against two of the jury.

At the end, Peacock said, 'Some cases throw up no leads, but this one shows every sign of having too many. Rather like a hunt where the fox's trails outnumber the hounds.' He gave Nick a sidelong glance. 'Cap that in French if you dare!'

CHAPTER FIVE

Vic Fielden looked about him with a self-important expression as he waited for the others to arrive the next morning. He felt he had become instantly recognisable as the foreman of the jury, one of whose members had been found murdered. Every time anyone happened to look in his direction, he was sure it was for this reason. His wife who had first spotted the news item in their morning paper had asked, with a tremor in her voice, whether it was safe for him to go to court that day, as though she envisaged the remaining eleven jurors being picked off one by one. Her husband did little to disabuse her of this notion, merely saying sternly that his public duty required him to be there.

As he stood waiting on the concourse outside the courtroom, he felt let down by the fact that none of the others had yet arrived. Surely they could have turned up early on such a morning.

Robert White was the first to appear and Vic made a bee-line for him, even though he was not one of his actual cronies.

'You've seen the terrible news?'

'About poor old Pewley, you mean?'

'Yes. I imagine it's in all the papers. Must have come as a special shock to you, seeing that you sat next to him in the box. I saw you talking together as we left one evening: I expect you got to know him better than some of the others?'

Mr White shrugged as though to indicate he found the conversation tasteless. 'I doubt it,' he said. 'I'm afraid I haven't regarded my jury service as an opportunity for social contact.' He paused before adding with a small chilly smile, 'As some have.'

Vic Fielden, however, was too strung up even to notice the reproof. 'I think we ought to club together for a wreath for his funeral,' he said, his mind racing ahead.

Before Mr White had a chance to comment, Fielden had turned to Ian Berenger who had just arrived.

'Terrible news, isn't it?'

'What news?' Berenger asked.

'About Laurence.'

'I haven't heard anything. Is he worse?'

'He's been found murdered.'

Berenger let out a startled whistle. 'So they really did mean business,' he said. 'The people behind the threats to Philip and David.'

Vic Fielden nodded grimly. 'I imagine we'll all have police protection from now on.'

'Surely you're not expecting the trial to continue?' This last remark came from Mr Brigstock, who had joined them a minute earlier. His tone carried a quiet note of authority. 'It can't possibly.'

'Why not? We sat yesterday with only eleven of us,' Berenger said.

Mr Brigstock threw him the sort of look a schoolmaster might accord an idiot intervention from one of his class.

'Because,' he replied slowly, 'I'd have thought it was obvious that the murder is connected with Mostyn's trial in some way and any police investigation must remain fettered so long as the trial goes on.'

Mr White gave a brief nod of agreement as Mr Brigstock looked round for support for his view.

'You mean you think Mostyn is behind Laurence's death?' Jim Dunn blurted out.

Lowering his voice, Mr Brigstock said testily, 'In view of what's happened already, that's obviously something the police'll have to investigate. And the point is that they can't so long as he's still on trial.'

'So what'll happen?'

Mr Brigstock gave an exasperated gulp as though wishing he had never made his intervention in the first place. 'What I imagine will happen is that the judge will discharge us and order a re-trial at some future date.'

'If that happens,' Vic Fielden said, asserting his own position, 'I suggest we meet over in that corner to discuss how we should pay our respects to Laurence's memory. I'm sure we'll want to send a wreath and I'll be glad to represent us all at his funeral.'

Mr Brigstock cast Robert White a surreptitious glance with eyebrows raised in scorn. 'And to think I'd always been a great believer in the jury system until I actually sat on one,' he observed.

As soon as they filed into court and took their places in the jury box, they could not fail to realise what a focus of interest they had suddenly become. Not only was the court fuller than usual, but everyone immediately looked in their direction as though they had assumed overnight a special aura. Embarrassed by the concentrated attention they attracted, most of them fixed their own looks on the court's inanimate trappings.

Amongst those subjecting them to special scrutiny was Detective Chief Superintendent Peacock who, accompanied by Detective Sergeant Nick Attwell, was sitting where he could take in everything that was happening. He had already seen the clerk of the court and been given a list of the jurors' names and addresses, and he had a team of well-briefed officers waiting to interview them as soon as the trial was officially abandoned.

He shifted his gaze from the jury and glanced at Bernie Mostyn, who was having an animated conversation with his solicitor. Detective Chief Inspector Scriven, who was sitting on one side of him and who had been busily scanning the scene, said suddenly, 'I don't see Ganci here today. He's one of Mostyn's strong-arm friends, known as Big G. He's been a fairly regular attender, but he's missing this morning. I'll have someone find out if there's anything significant about that.'

Peacock nodded as his glance roamed on to where counsel were sitting. Gilbert Trapp Q.C. was a large, rather portly man with a florid face. He tended towards pomposity and had a rich voice, whose sound clearly pleased him. His junior, Malcolm Edland, was also on the far side, but was a much jollier looking person in every way. Robin Culshaw, the prosecuting counsel, was huddled in his seat as though trying to escape notice. He was an accomplished advocate and someone who managed to impart a sense of style to almost everything he undertook. Nothing ever surprised him, not even the murder of a juror in one of his trials. He simply moved on, without fuss, to the next case on his agenda.

Peacock had just brought his gaze back to the jury when knocks on the door indicated the arrival of Judge Slingsby. The accompanying ceremonial was performed as though nothing untoward had occurred. As Nick reflected, it took more than a murdered juror to ruffle the majesty of the law.

When everyone was seated, the judge glanced towards the jury and then addressed himself to counsel.

'Mr Culshaw and Mr Trapp, as you may already be aware, the juror, with whose presence we dispensed yesterday morning in the belief that he had been taken ill, has been found dead in circumstances which call for a police investigation. It seems to me that, in the course of their enquiries, the police will in all likelihood wish to interview people who are concerned with this trial – some of his fellow jurors, for example – and that the continuation of the trial must therefore of necessity inhibit such an investigation. I have therefore decided that I have no alternative but to discharge the jury from returning a verdict and to order that the accused shall stand trial on this indictment at some future date.'

As Judge Slingsby had already discussed the situation with counsel in his room before the court sat, his formal pronouncement was less for their benefit than for the press and, through it, the world at large.

Robin Culshaw merely gave the judge a short bow, murmured, 'As your lordship pleases,' and sat down again.

Gilbert Trapp, however, clasped his hands across his chest and gave an appearance of being about to deliver an oration.

'I would like, my lord, to express on behalf of myself, my instructing solicitors and my client our deepest sympathy with the family of the dead man and to assure the police that we are available to assist them in their enquiries as required. I think, my lord, that in fairness to my client, I must make it emphatically clear that he has been stunned and shocked by the news of this juror's untimely death as anyone in court. He ...'

'I think, Mr Trapp,' the judge broke in, 'that the less said on this occasion, the better.'

'My lord, if I may say so with great respect, I entirely agree with your lordship's sentiments. I must, however, crave your lordship's indulgence to refer to one other aspect of your lordship's decision. Mr Mostyn has had this matter hanging over his head for several months and now through no fault of his the period of worry and anxiety is to be prolonged.'

'Never heard such a load of cock! And with legal knobs on!' Scriven muttered into Nick's ear. 'Bernie's only worry is being convicted and sent down. They wouldn't let him wear his vicuna coat in prison.'

'I thought it only right to bring that aspect to your lordship's notice,' Mr Trapp concluded, glaring in Scriven's direction. He had caught the word 'cock' which had displeased him.

'Thank you, Mr Trapp,' Judge Slingsby said briskly. Then turning to the jury, he went on, 'Members of the jury, I am sorry that we part with this case in such unhappy circumstances. I understand that the police would like to speak to you before you leave the precincts and so I would ask you to retire to your room where an officer will have a word with you. Finally, I should like to thank you for your diligence and attention during the past ten days.'

The judge rose, as did Mr Trapp.

'My lord, there is the question of bail. I take it your lordship will release my client on his existing bail pending his re-trial.'

'Yes, indeed.'

'I am much obliged to your lordship.'

As people made for the various exits, the jury filed off to their room in the wake of an usher with Peacock and Nick bringing up the rear.

'I'm Detective Chief Superintendent Peacock and this is Detective Sergeant Attwell,' Peacock began as soon as they were in the jury room and the usher had retired. 'As you probably know, Mr Pewley was murdered. I know the judge put it less bluntly in court, but that's because the law always wraps everything up in elegant words. Nastily and cruelly murdered he was and it is my belief that his death was in some way related to this case you've been on. At all events, the dead man spent the last days of his life in your daily company and so it's only natural that I should come to you first and seek your help. I don't want to keep you here longer than necessary, but in a few minutes, my officers and I will be interviewing each one of you in turn. Some of you probably have more to tell us than others. For example' – he glanced down at a piece of paper he was holding – 'I shall want to get the full story of the earlier incidents involving Mr Davey and Mr Weir. I should like each one of you gentlemen to cudgel your brains for any scrap of information you can give us about Mr Pewley. However small and unimportant it may seem to you, please tell us. Many a case has been solved by a seemingly trivial and insignificant item.'

As Peacock paused, Vic Fielden who had been itching to speak seized his opportunity.

'As foreman of this jury, I'm sure I speak for everyone when I say we'll all assist you in any way we can. We are deeply sensible of the tragedy which has befallen our colleague, Laurence Pewley, and I know that each of us will regard it as a duty to help in the search for his murderer.'

One or two jurors nodded, a few looked embarrassed by Fielden's little speech and others remained impassive. Only Mr Brigstock said anything and that was in an aside to Mr White.

'Now he's an *ex*-foreman of jury, it's time he shut up. I don't need him to show me where my duty lies.'

'Thank you, sir,' Peacock said gravely. 'And now if you'll wait in this room, we'll fetch you one by one for interview.'

Vic Fielden, who had been disappointed that his little speech was not accorded ringing support by his colleagues, was now mollified by being asked to accompany Peacock to the interview room ahead of the others.

In fact, Peacock had allotted himself Fielden, Davey and Weir, as on the information available it seemed likely they could say more than the others.

Nick had Mr White at the top of his list and they now faced one another across a small table in a cell-like room.

'May I start by asking your full name, Mr White?' Nick said with a smile which seemed to apologise for the clichéed beginning.

'Robert White.'

'Just *Robert* White?'

'Yes, my parents were strictly practical people and didn't believe in giving their children a lot of names which would never be used.'

'And your address?'

'Twenty-seven A, Hilltop Drive, Barnes.'

'Your occupation?'

'Company director.'

Nick, who had recorded these particulars, laid down his pen and rubbed a finger.

'Was this your first time on a jury?' he enquired in a conversational tone.

'Yes. And my last, I hope.'

'You haven't enjoyed the experience then?'

'As far as I'm concerned, it's been a waste of valuable time.'

'You didn't get any satisfaction out of performing a public duty?'

Mr White gave him a quick glance as if to check whether he was being serious.

'I can't say I did,' he replied with a shrug, 'though some of the others appeared to.'

'Of course porn cases are not everyone's choice.'

'That didn't bother me.'

Nick, who had been asking his questions rather as a T.V. personality warms up the studio audience before the show begins, now picked up his pen again.

'I believe you sat next to the dead man in the jury box?'

'Yes.'

'With Mr Davey on his other side?'

'Yes.'

'And you sat at the end of the row so that there was no one on your other side?'

'Correct.'

'Did you have much conversation with Mr Pewley in the course of the trial?'

'Not much.'

'Do you recall speaking to him when the court rose on the evening before he disappeared?'

'If I did speak to him, I don't recall anything special about it. I think it may have been that evening or the previous one that we happened to walk down the staircase together.'

'Yes?'

Mr White looked at Nick sharply. 'That's all there was to it. We just happened to find ourselves side by side as we left.'

'Did Mr Pewley ever tell you anything about himself?'

'I think he mentioned that he lived alone and I got the impression from something he said that he used to call in at his place of work most evenings after court.'

'Did he ever say anything about his work?'

'Nothing to me.'

'What sort of impression did you form of him?'

'I didn't.'

'Oh, surely you must have formed some impression?' Nick said in a coaxing tone.

Mr White shrugged. 'I don't think we'd ever have become bosom friends.'

'You didn't care for him, in fact?'

'I suppose not.'

'What was it about him that put you off?'

'He just wasn't my sort of person.'

'Did he ever reveal anything about himself which put you off him?'

'No. It was just that I didn't take to him.' He paused. 'He wasn't the only one. There were several of them I didn't care for.'

'How would you sum him up?'

Mr White frowned at the table before replying. Then with another shrug, he said, 'To be quite frank, I thought he was the sort of person one could find round the Soho strip clubs.'

'That's very interesting! Did he ever give any indication that he frequented those sort of places?'

'Not to me.'

'It was just an impression?'

'Purely an impression.'

'How did his appearance strike you?'

'How do you mean?' Mr White's tone held a note of suspicion.

'His hair, for example?'

'What about it?'

'Did it strike you as unusual in any way?'

'A lot of people wear their hair long these days, even men of his sort of age.'

Nick glanced at Mr White's head of well trimmed silvery grey hair. He was obviously someone who had gone grey prematurely and there was no indication what colour his hair had been before.

'It never occurred to you that he wore a wig?' Nick asked.

'Did he?' Nick nodded. 'No, it didn't! Well, I'll be damned! I suppose it was because it was long at the back that one didn't notice the gap between hair and neck.'

'You don't know whether any of the other jurors noticed?'

'No idea! It's not the sort of thing one discusses.'

'Someone might have mentioned it.'

'Not to me.'

Nick studied what he had written down. After a pause, he went on, 'Did the dead man ever give you any indication that he had been threatened or intimidated in the course of the trial?'

'None ... Well, no, not really. He certainly never said anything to suggest that.'

'But you nevertheless had that impression?' Nick urged.

Mr White shifted uncomfortably on his chair as though wishing he had not brought the matter up. Eventually, he said, 'There was a man who used to come into court quite often, a friend of the defendant's. At least, I assume so as I saw them talking together on more than one occasion outside the court. I was almost certain that once when he was sitting in court, he was staring straight at Pewley as though to try and attract his attention and that Pewley seemed equally determined not to catch his eye. After that I used to watch this chap whenever he came into court and though it was never quite as obvious again, I had a feeling that he used to focus his attention deliberately on Pewley.'

'What did this man look like?'

'A big man. Well over six feet tall and tough-looking.'

'Chucker-out type?'

'Exactly.'

'And what sort of look did he give the dead man?'

'Just a hard, cold stare.'

'An intimidating sort of stare?'

'Coming from him, I'd say yes.'

A few minutes later, Mr White had signed the statement which Nick had recorded and had left after Nick had thanked him for his help.

The next person on his list for interview was Jim Dunn, who, despite a boyish eagerness to help, had, it soon became clear, little to offer the enquiry. Nick had the impression that he was the sort of amiable young man who drifted with the crowd. He certainly couldn't see him exerting any influence as a juror, the majority view would have been good enough for him to go along with.

He told Nick that he had found most of his fellow jurors a decent lot including Mr Pewley. He gave a nervous giggle when Nick asked him if he'd been aware that the dead man wore a wig and said that he thought it might have been as once he had accidentally caught up a lock of his hair in a paper clip on some documents they'd been handed – he'd been sitting immediately behind Mr Pewley – without Pewley noticing.

Dunn was replaced by Mr Brigstock who made it quite clear that he was cross at having been kept waiting.

'It's a pity you didn't first find out which of us had important business elsewhere,' he said tartly to Nick's mild apology for the slowness of the proceedings. Nick forbore to point out that he had presumably arrived at court in the expectation of spending the whole day there, as it was apparent that Mr Brigstock's resentment arose through not having been accorded priority over others.

He made it clear that he had not been favourably impressed by the majority of his fellow jurors and he dismissed Vic Fielden as 'that soap-powder salesman'. He made no bones about his dislike of the dead man and seemed to share Mr White's view of his propensities, as evidenced by his obvious enjoyment of the material they had spent a day reading in the jury room.

When it came to Mr Pewley's hair, he told Nick that he assumed it was dyed as he had never seen a man with that tint before. It was like a girl's hair, he had added. When told that it was, in fact, a wig, he let out a disdainful snort.

'I should have thought they'd be well advised to review the qualifications for jury service,' he said, as the interview came to a close. 'No wonder so many criminals get off these days!' And with this enigmatic comment he had departed.

It was early afternoon by the time all eleven jurors had been interviewed and Peacock and his officers met to exchange notes. A large pot of tea and a couple of plates of sandwiches had been put on the table round which they sat.

For a time they ate in silence while Peacock read through the bundle of statements which had been collected and put in front of him. When he had finished, he questioned them in turn about their respective interviews.

Looking towards Nick, he said, 'This fellow whom White refers to as giving Pewley the evil eye is probably Ganci. I gather from Scriven that he was in and out of court a good deal.'

'Did any of the others mention that, sir?' Nick asked.

'Davey had noticed Ganci in court and wondered whether he was the muscle-man who had barged him off the pavement when he was going home that evening. But I gather he was only going on size, as he never saw the man's face in the dark.'

'It would fit, wouldn't it, sir? A spot of aggro applied out of court and someone like Ganci beaming a few meaningful stares at the jury in court.'

'But they weren't at the jury as a whole,' Peacock said, 'they appear to have been reserved for friend Pewley.'

'I wonder if he'd been got at by the defence,' Nick said in a musing tone. 'If so, Ganci's evil eye on him in court would be to remind him to stay in line.'

Peacock nodded. 'That'll be one of our first lines of enquiry. Had Pewley been nobbled?' He leafed thoughtfully through the eleven statements before him. 'Incidentally,' he went on, 'this fellow Davey who sat on Pewley's other side seems to have been very struck by the fact he always brought a briefcase to court, but was never seen to open it. He apparently kept it with him all the time, even taking it up to the jury cafeteria at lunchtime when the rest of them left their personal bits and pieces in court.' He paused. 'I don't know that I attach great importance to it, but Davey seems to have thought there was something unusual about it.'

'What would he have wanted to bring a briefcase to court for?' Nick asked.

'And not open it,' added someone else.

'That's what puzzled Davey.'

Peacock got up. 'Come on, Nick, we're going to Pewley's place of work. I want to find out a bit more about him before we tackle Bernie Mostyn.'

'Wonder if I might make a phone call, first, sir?'

'To Woman Detective Constable Reynolds by any chance?'

Nick grinned. 'As a matter of fact, yes, sir.'

'My compliments to Clare and tell her she won't be seeing her fiancé this evening.'

'That was what I was proposing to tell her, sir.'

CHAPTER SIX

Eve Place was a short alley off the old section of London Wall. At its far end lay the offices of Messrs Tuke and Wirrall, quantity surveyors.

When Peacock and Nick arrived, they were taken straight up to the office of the senior partner whose name was Hutchinson. With him, also awaiting their arrival, was a Mr Tetley, who was introduced as the office manager.

'What a shocking business this is!' Mr Hutchinson declared as soon as they were all seated. 'Of all the harmless, inoffensive people, Mr Pewley couldn't ever have hurt anyone in his life. And to think he met this dreadful end as a result of performing a civic duty! It really is too awful for words.'

'How long had he been in your employ?'

'Eight years. And a most valuable employee he was.'

'What was his particular job?'

'He was a clerk in our accounts section.'

'Where he worked with others?'

'With three or four others, all considerably younger.'

'Was he in charge of them?'

'Oh no. They were all equal in that sense, although he'd been here longer than any of them. Miss Crawford is our chief accountant. She's responsible for the work of the section.' Mr Hutchinson gave a small heave in the act of suppressing a belch and quickly popped a tablet into his mouth. 'His great value to us,' he went on, 'was his quite remarkable memory. He was the nearest thing to a human computer you could find. You didn't need to refer to records when he was around, he had it all in his head.' He turned to Mr Tetley. 'That was so, wasn't it, Arthur?'

Mr Tetley nodded. 'Yes, indeed. He was almost like that memory man who used to be on the radio.'

'What other things did he have stored in his mind apart from office matters?' Peacock asked with an expression of faint incredulity.

'Virtually anything he'd ever read or been told.'

'Remarkable.'

'He really was! The number of times he came to the firm's rescue because he could remember some transaction or other everyone else had forgotten was incredible. I don't mind telling you it often saved us hours searching through old records.'

'Was he popular with the staff?' Peacock asked.

Mr Hutchinson glanced towards Mr Tetley.

'You have closer contact with staff than I, Arthur, so you can probably answer that better.'

'He wasn't unpopular,' Mr Tetley said in a cautious tone. 'He certainly wasn't a hail-fellow, well-met type of person.'

'But as far as you know, he didn't have any enemies within the firm?'

'Good lord, no! As Mr Hutchinson has said, he was a most inoffensive man.'

'You know of nobody who might have wished to kill him?'

'Certainly not!'

'I gather from something said by one of his fellow jurors that he used to come into the office after the court had risen. That's so, is it?'

'Not every evening, but he'd been looking in about twice a week.'

'Who would have seen him on those occasions?'

'The persons in his own section.'

'Neither of you gentlemen saw him then?'

Mr Hutchinson shook his head and Mr Tetley said, 'I saw him briefly one evening. I just asked him how he was enjoying himself on the jury and he said he was finding it interesting. That was all the conversation we had.'

'As you may have seen from the press, he was found without any hair. Were you aware that he wore a wig?'

'I think it may have crossed my mind,' Mr Hutchinson said, 'but it wasn't something I gave thought to. One gets used to someone's appearance and accepts it without, so to speak, noticing it. There was nothing particular about Mr Pewley's appearance. He was the sort of person who could melt into a background without any difficulty. Wouldn't you agree, Arthur?'

'Yes. Frankly, I hadn't noticed he wore a wig until I heard two of the youngsters in his section speculating about it. I'm afraid they were having a bet on it. It was certainly a very well made one.'

'Though a bit trendy for someone his age, don't you think?'

'I wouldn't have said there was anything trendy about mouse-coloured hair.'

'Ah! That's what I was wondering. He wore his short, mouse-coloured hairpiece at work, did he?'

'Do you mean he had others?' Mr Tetley asked, incredulously.

'At least three others. All different.'

'But why?'

'I can't tell you. Vanity in his personal appearance, I suppose. We do know that he wore a much fuller wig of chestnut coloured hair while he was on the jury.'

'Good gracious!'

'When you saw him that evening back here, Mr Tetley, what was he wearing then?'

'It must have been the one he always wore in the office or I'd have noticed.'

'Could explain the briefcase,' Peacock said to Nick, who nodded. He turned back to the other two. 'Did you know anything about his home life?'

'Nothing. Not that there's anything unusual about that. We're not a paternalistic firm: we don't interest ourselves in the private lives of our staff. Though,' Mr Hutchinson added quickly, 'that doesn't mean we're not ready to help anyone in domestic trouble if called on to do so. We're not soulless, either.'

'Did Pewley have any close friends in the office?'

'No.' This time it was Mr Tetley who answered.

'Who knew him best?'

'I suppose Miss Crawford.'

'Perhaps I could have a word with her before we leave?'

'I'm afraid she's not in this week. She has flu.'

'Then I'd like to have a talk to some of his colleagues in the accounts section.'

'Certainly. Mr Tetley can take you down there now, if there's nothing further I can help you with for the time being.'

The accounts section was housed in a semi-basement room where the lights had to be switched on even on the lightest day of summer. When Mr Tetley and his visitors entered, its two occupants were chatting over in a corner. One was sitting at a desk and the other was perched on it. Neither of them looked older than his early twenties. Mr Tetley introduced them as Mr Barrow and Mr Sanderson. After acknowledging the two visitors with small nods, they looked at Peacock and Nick with guarded expressions.

'I don't think we need detain you, Mr Tetley,' Peacock said. 'One of these young gentlemen can show us where to find you when we've finished.'

Mr Tetley appeared faintly nonplussed but, after a second's hesitation, left the room. When he had gone, Peacock glanced about the room while its two young occupants continued to watch him with wary expressions.

'Where did Pewley sit?' he asked at length.

'That desk there,' Barrow said, indicating one nearest the radiator.

'How long have you worked here?'

'A couple of years.'

'In the accounts section the whole time?'

'Apart from the first month, yes.'

'And you?' he asked, looking at Sanderson.

'Just under twelve months.'

'Who's the fourth person in this room? Miss Crawford?'

'No, she has a room to herself. It's Mr Mason. Or rather it was Mr Mason. He left about a month ago and hasn't been replaced yet.'

'So it was just you two and Pewley in this room?'

'Correct.'

'What sort of person was he?'

Barrow made a face and looked at Sanderson who pushed out his lower lip and shrugged.

'Difficult to say really,' Sanderson said after an awkward silence.

'I gather neither of you liked him that much,' Peacock observed.

'He wasn't too bad a chap, poor old Flo!' Barrow said.

'Flo! Was that what you called him?'

They both nodded. 'Not to his face, mind you,' Barrow added.

'Why Flo?'

'Short for Florence.'

'I realise that, but why Florence?'

'He always signed himself F. Laurence Pewley.'

'Did the nickname "Flo" reflect your feelings about him?'

'I suppose it did in a way.'

'You found him a figure of fun?'

The two exchanged an embarrassed look. Then Sanderson said, 'Let's tell them, shall we, Clive?' Barrow nodded and Sanderson went on, 'If you really want to know, we found him a real little creep.'

'In what way?' Peacock asked in an encouraging tone.

'In practically every way,' Barrow said. 'He was sly and two-faced and smutty. A real creep he was, just like Doug says.'

Peacock glanced from one to the other with the absorbed expression of a quizmaster.

'Let's take the last bit first. In what way was he smutty?'

'Always making insinuating remarks about sex and trying to find out how many girls we'd laid and things like that.'

'And you also described him as two-faced.'

'He was, too.' This time it was Sanderson who spoke. 'He'd pretend to be on our side against old Tetley and then we'd discover he'd been saying things about us behind our backs. Sneaky things!'

'How did he get on with Miss Crawford?'

'I think she saw through him as well as anyone, but she also recognised his value to the firm.'

'We've been told he had a remarkable memory.'

'Fantastic, it was,' Barrow said. 'There's no disputing that. It was quite fantastic, wasn't it, Doug?'

'Yes. That was what added to his creepiness.'

'I gather you knew he wore a wig.'

'His hair was always exactly the same length and occasionally when he thought no one was watching, he'd stick a pencil underneath to scratch his scalp.'

'Did he always wear the same one?'

'The one with short mousey hair. Never saw him wear any other, but Clive and I used to wonder if he carried a spare in his briefcase. He was never without it—his briefcase, I mean—but he never opened it when anyone was around. So heaven knows what he did carry in it if it wasn't a spare wig!'

'I don't quite follow,' Nick broke in, 'why you should have assumed there was a spare wig in it?'

'We had absolutely no evidence of it at all,' Barrow said. 'It's simply that we used to speculate about him, particularly about how he spent his evenings, and we built a sort of fantasy life for him in which he went off to seedy clubs and blue film shows.'

'Wearing a different wig for each occasion?'

'That sort of thing,' Barrow acknowledged with an embarrassed smile.

'You mayn't have been far wrong,' Peacock observed in a sardonic tone.

'You mean, he really was like that?'

'It's a bit too soon to tie any definite labels on him, but he was an odd cove from all accounts.'

And that's putting it mildly, Nick reflected as he watched Peacock abstractedly clean a fingernail with the thumbnail of his other hand.

'When was the last occasion either of you saw Pewley?' Peacock went on, after an apparently satisfactory inspection of the nail concerned.

'He looked in the evening before last. About half past four,' Barrow said.

'How long did he stay?'

'He was still here when I left at five.'

Peacock glanced at Sanderson, who shook his head. 'I didn't see him that evening. I was upstairs with Mr Noakes, one of the partners.'

'What sort of mood was he in?' Peacock asked, returning his gaze to Barrow.

'Well, that's the funny thing, he seemed particularly pleased with himself.'

'Was that unusual?'

'No, he was often that way, particularly when he had pulled off one of his little coups, like remembering something everyone else had forgotten or scoring off one of the staff. But on this occasion, he was all mysterious as well. He kept on rubbing his hands together in a gleeful manner and he said something about bread.'

'Bread?'

'Yes. Something about fetching bread, I think it was.'

'You didn't ask him what he meant?'

'I'm afraid not. It was so obvious he wanted me to that I was determined not to.'

'You reacted against his mood?'

'We usually did.'

'Pity,' Peacock said with a sigh. 'However, can you run through everything you remember of that evening from the time he arrived at about half past four?'

'He came in, carrying his briefcase, and called out, "Good evening to you, Clive" as soon as he was inside the door. I just looked up and said "Hello" in a not very enthusiastic tone. And then he went across to his desk and glanced at the papers on it. He was humming all this time, which was a sure sign he was feeling pleased with himself. A short time later when I got up, he asked me if I was going out with my girl that evening and when I made some non-committal answer, he rubbed his hands together like I said and remarked that he was going after some bread.'

'Did he say "fetch" or "going after"?'

'I can't really be sure he said either. All I'm certain of was he used the word "bread".'

'Had he ever talked about bread before?'

'No.'

'And you weren't curious?'

'Mildly so, but I wasn't going to let him see.'

'He may have said "bread" meaning money,' Sanderson put in.

Peacock nodded. 'I didn't imagine he was referring to a loaf,' he said in a tone which caused Sanderson to blush. 'Did he often talk in riddles?' he asked, looking back to Barrow.

'Not often, but it wasn't unknown. It was all part of his quirkiness.'

There was a silence while Peacock picked at another nail. Then looking up, he said suddenly, 'Did either of you ever get any suggestion that he was blackmailing someone?'

They both shook their heads and Sanderson said, 'But I'd never have been surprised to hear that he was.'

'Because you found him a generally creepy person?'

'Correct.'

'Did he ever show signs of having more money than he earned here?'

'He certainly didn't throw his money around, if that's what you mean. I'd say he was ultra careful with his money, wouldn't you, Clive?'

Barrow nodded. 'Never stood either of us so much as a cup of tea.'

Peacock glanced at Nick. 'Anything else you can think of?'

'Would anyone have seen him leave when he departed the evening before last?'

'George. He's our head messenger and he locks up after everyone has gone. He's a widower and has a tiny flat at the back.'

'I think we ought to have a word with him, sir,' Nick said.

'Can one of you fetch him?' Peacock said.

A couple of minutes later, Clive Barrow returned with a small, leathery looking man with a bald head who was wearing a commissionaire's uniform with a row of medals on his chest.

''Evening, guvnor,' he said, looking at Peacock. ''Evening, sarge,' he added, giving Nick a brisk nod of the head. 'What is it you want to know?'

'Did you see Pewley leave the evening before last?'

'That was the last time he was here. Yes, I saw him

leave, guvnor. It was between a quarter and half past five.'

'Did you speak to him?'

'Only said "good-night" like.'

'Was he alone?'

'As far as I recall, he was alone.'

'Where were you at the time?'

'By the main entrance where I always am at that hour.'

'And there was nothing about him to attract your attention?'

'Nothing, guvnor.'

Nick had the impression that George hadn't had much time for Mr Pewley, which was not perhaps surprising given their obvious differences.

'How long have you worked here, George?'

'Fifteen years.'

'So you've known Pewley ever since he's been with the firm?'

'There's some you get to know, guvnor, others you don't get to know, and others you don't want to get to know. Pewley tried to get me into trouble once and after that I had no use for him. Not that I had much before!'

'How long ago was that?'

'It wasn't long after he came. A good few years back now.' He glanced at Barrow and Sanderson. 'Long before these two young gents joined the firm.'

Nick made a mental note to ask Mr Tetley what the trouble had been, not that it was likely to prove relevant to their present enquiry. In fact, the opportunity came about a quarter of an hour later when they were leaving and Mr Tetley was bidding them farewell at the door. A frown of faint annoyance crossed his brow when Nick raised the matter.

'Oh, dear,' he said, 'I hope all our little office tiffs are not going to be raked over. I assure you the incident in question is long over and forgotten and the fact that both the persons concerned remained in our employ is evidence of its trivial nature. What happened was that Mr Pewley brought it to the notice of one of the partners that George had been drinking in office hours.'

'And had he?'

'I think he'd had a glass of beer, but that was all. He certainly wasn't drunk or anything like that.'

'Shows Pewley to have been a bit of a busybody,' Peacock observed.

'Perhaps he was inclined that way at times,' Mr Tetley said guardedly. 'But I can assure you that his good qualities far outweighed his ... his less good ones.'

As they walked back down the alley to where their car was parked, Peacock said, 'One invariably learns more from the lower orders than from the top ranks on these occasions. Those two young lads in the accounts section gave us a far better picture of Pewley than Messrs Hutchinson and Tetley.' He paused. 'Flo! Tells one everything about him in three letters!'

The drive back to their murder headquarters was largely silent. It was only as they were nearing the Station that Peacock suddenly asked, 'Shall we find Woman Detective Constable Reynolds on duty when we get back?'

Nick was always suspicious when his Detective Chief Superintendent referred to his fiancée rather laboriously by her full title as it often presaged one of his unfunnier turns of mind. Indeed, Nick had never been able to decide just how Peacock did view his engagement to Clare. At times he seemed benign, even paternal, but then he could suddenly show an insensitivity, amounting almost to malice.

'Yes, sir,' Nick replied in a neutral tone.

'Well, I have just the job for her. To sift through all those cuttings Pewley kept and make out a schedule.'

'I'll tell her, sir,' Nick said, with a feeling of relief.

'And then you and I will do a smart turn around and go and seek out Bernie Mostyn.'

CHAPTER SEVEN

Nick found Clare interviewing an eight-year-old girl who had been assaulted by her step-father. 'Interviewing', though, was perhaps not quite the right description as when he stuck his head round the door, they were having a game of noughts and crosses, while the child's mother watched with a perplexed expression.

Clare smiled when she saw Nick at the door. 'I'm almost through if you want me.'

'Can't we have another game, miss?' the child said urgently. 'I'll win next time.'

'All right, one more.' Clare glanced back at Nick. 'I don't know why Polly says *next* time. She's won almost every time. I certainly chose the wrong game when I suggested noughts and crosses.'

Nick grinned and watched the small girl with her absorbed expression as she proceeded deftly to win again.

'I'll just see Mrs Anson and Polly out and then I'll be with you,' Clare said as she and the girl and her mother got up.

Five minutes later she came into the room where he was waiting for her and walked over and kissed him.

'It's all right, no one's looking,' she said brightly, aware of his reserve about displays of affection in the office.

'If the guvnor ever saw us kissing in the C.I.D., it'd be the salt mines for both of us.'

'I'm always very discreet,' she said with a happy smile. 'Anyway, I bet I could get round old Peacock.'

Though he was the last person to underrate his fiancée's charms, Nick was less sure about the Detective Chief

Superintendent's susceptibility to feminine wiles, even Clare's.

'In any event, I expect he knows or, at least, he guesses,' she added.

'There's a world of difference between guessing and knowing.'

Clare's only comment on this was to kiss him again. Then moving swiftly round to the other side of his desk, she said, 'I understand you wanted to see me, Sergeant.'

Nick grinned. 'The guvnor has a job for you on our murder enquiry.' And he went on to give her a run-down on their discoveries to date.

'What an awful little creep he sounds!' Clare said when he had finished. 'Clearly not much loss to society.'

'I agree, but we still have to try as hard to find his murderer as if he were the hero of the hour.'

'I know! So you want me to itemise all these newspaper cuttings?'

'That's the idea. I suggest you put an asterisk against the most promising ones, such as those relating to the Soho vice scene. And, of course, if you happened to turn up anything concerning Mostyn, let me know immediately.'

'Fine, I'll start right away.'

'The guvnor and I want to interview him this evening.'

'Are you bringing him here?'

'No, we're going to try and catch him at one of his places.'

'So I mayn't see you again today?'

'Probably not.'

'Well, take care, my darling. Remember, there are more important things in heaven and on earth than catching murderers, namely keeping yourself intact to marry me next June.'

'I can't forget that.'

She was about to come round the desk and kiss him again, when the door opened to reveal Peacock.

'Ah!' he exclaimed, 'I hope I don't interrupt your conference.'

Nick always found it difficult to react suitably to such heavily jocular sallies, but Clare responded without any sign of embarrassment.

'Nick was just telling me, sir, that you want me to go through the dead man's books of newspaper cuttings.'

When she was speaking to Peacock, she always referred to her fiancé as Nick. In the very early days of their engagement, he had once pointedly asked if she meant Sergeant Attwell and she had retorted politely but with considerable firmness that it was unnatural and, in her view, unnecessary to refer to him so formally when they were speaking together. After which, he had left the subject alone.

'That's right. It's a job that needs a woman's thoroughness. I have a feeling there are all sorts of clues buried amongst those cuttings.'

'Does that mean, sir, you don't associate his death with serving on the Mostyn jury?'

Peacock stared at her with an abstracted expression.

'No-o, it doesn't mean that,' he said slowly. 'I'm sure his death is connected with the Mostyn case, but I don't know how. The fact that two jurors were intimidated and then a third gets killed means that there must be some connection. Equally, the fact that Pewley was the person he was must also be relevant.' He paused. 'This is really no more than thinking aloud, but what I feel is that, whereas Davey and Weir were picked at random for intimidation, Pewley was not. In some way he was more involved. It wasn't just a logical progression of telephone threats, as in Weir's case, mild physical violence, as in Davey's, and, finally, murder, because that doesn't make sense. After all, you don't need to resort to the extreme of murder in order to nobble a jury. So the motive for Flo's murder has to be something other than that. Nevertheless, I'm damned sure it's something connected with the particular trial.' He glanced at Nick. 'Agreed?'

'The trouble about Flo's death, sir, is that, unlike most, it has thrown up a surfeit of clues. There are too many trails to follow, instead of too few. It seems to me that the intimidation of the first two jurors may have been a smokescreen to divert us from what was already planned, namely the murder of Flo.'

'Well, go on,' Peacock said, when Nick stopped.

'That's all, sir. I was merely indicating that we have ... have ...'

'What do we have?'

Nick grinned sheepishly. 'What the French, sir, call *un embarras de choix*! An embarrassment of choice.'

Peacock's eyes opened a fraction wider as he stared coolly at Nick. Then turning to Clare, he said, 'I hope you'll remember to take a French dictionary to bed with you when you're married to him, otherwise you won't know what he's talking about.'

'I'll remember to do that, sir,' Clare replied with a deadpan expression. There were times when it was better not to try and cap Peacock's laboured humour. Indeed, it was only really safe to do so when he made it clear that this was what he expected. On occasions such as the present he was liable to jump in the opposite direction if, mistaking the signs, you entered into the spirit of what you took to be a jesting mood. As Nick had more than once observed, 'He can be a perverse old cuss, but I still like him.' A sentiment which Clare shared.

'Well, now that we've had our French lesson for today, perhaps we'd better get on with more immediate things, such as a visit to the Petronella Club where, with luck, we'll find Bernie Mostyn and some of his friends. Ready?'

'Ready, sir.'

'And you get on with your bit of homework, Clare. And I'm not referring to your fiancé either!'

As Peacock turned to go out of the door, Nick rolled his eyes heavenwards in an expression of despair. He sometimes wondered from where Peacock culled his humour. Probably from years of watching the comperes of corny quiz programmes on television, he usually decided.

He blew Clare a quick kiss as he followed his Detective Chief Superintendent out of the room.

CHAPTER EIGHT

The Petronella Club off Greek Street was no different from a dozen or more similar institutions in the teeming square mile of Soho, which catered for the visitor with a roll of banknotes to be got rid of and the habitué whose motive was more devious.

A green neon sign proclaimed its existence with a flashing arrow which pointed at a shiny black door.

It was a few minutes after six o'clock when Peacock and Nick arrived. Nick gave the door a push but, when it held, he pressed the bell at one side. A flap opened to reveal a pair of eyes and a nose.

'The club's not open,' the owner of the features said in an uncompromising tone.

'We're police. We want to talk to Bernie.'

'I'll see if he's here,' the voice said before closing the flap.

Peacock, who was standing just behind Nick, began to hum in a tuneless fashion.

'You don't think he'll try and avoid seeing us, sir?'

Peacock shook his head. 'He'll see us all right. Probably expecting us. Just a matter of going through the formalities.'

He had barely finished speaking when the door opened and the same man said, 'It's O.K., Bernie's free.'

'I like that expression, "Bernie's free",' Peacock remarked to Nick in an amiable aside. 'What's your name?' he asked of the man who had admitted them.

'Les Duke.'

''Evening, Les. Lead on.'

The short passage gave way to a staircase leading to the basement. Half-way down the stairs made a right-angle turn, one side clinging to a plain brick wall, the other open to the room below. Watching them as they descended were Bernie Mostyn and Big G Ganci. They were sitting at a table tucked against one end of a small chromium bar. The only other man in the room was the barman, who appeared to be in the act of washing glasses but who was evincing a much greater interest in the arrival of the visitors.

Apart from concealed lighting at the back of the bar, there was no illumination. Between the foot of the staircase and the bar was a dance floor not much larger than a dining-room table and over in a farther corner, strangely silent for once, lurked a discothèque.

Mostyn got up as the officers approached his table.

'Saw you in court this morning,' he said affably, 'but Les didn't tell me your name.'

'Probably because I didn't tell *him*,' Peacock observed drily. 'I'm Detective Chief Superintendent Peacock and this is Detective Sergeant Attwell.'

'Move your arse over so our friends can sit down,' Mostyn said to Ganci who had remained lounging back in his chair.

Ganci moved as if he had been suddenly stung.

'What are you drinking, Mr Peacock?' Mostyn asked when they were all seated.

'Scotch.'

'Sergeant?'

'The same, please.'

'A round of scotches, Carlo, and don't take all evening. He's new,' he added to Peacock, as though an explanation was called for. 'Last fellow developed a thirst himself and had to go.' Their drinks arrived and Mostyn raised his glass. 'Here's to the police despite all the aggro they give me!'

'I've come to get your help, not add to the aggro,' Peacock said.

'If that's true, it'll be a change. It's been a constant harassment these past few years. I reckon it's probably easier to earn a living in Russia than in London these days.'

'Depends on the sort of living, doesn't it, Bernie? From all accounts, you don't do too badly. Holidays in Cyprus and Jamaica already this year. An American car as big as the *Q.E.2* and a house in fashionable Finchley.'

Mostyn, who had listened to this précis of his affluence with half-closed eyes, gave a non-committal grunt at the end.

'And now look what's happened over this bloody trial,' he said angrily. 'I spend the last ten bloody days growing corns on my arse at the Old Bailey only to have to face the whole thing starting all over again. It's unjust: not to mention what it's costing me. If you don't call that aggro ...'

'Not as much aggro to you as it was to that juror who's been murdered.'

'I don't know a bloody thing about that. Why should it have to be a juror at my trial who gets himself strangled?'

'You've taken the very words out of my mouth,' Peacock said blandly.

'Well, I tell you again, I don't know a bloody thing about his death.'

Peacock nodded impatiently as though to indicate that the sooner they dispensed with the expected formal denials, the better they would get on.

'I gather you challenged your full quota of jurors before the trial started?' he said.

'My brief did. I didn't,' Mostyn said with a frown.

'Was it on your instructions?'

'No, it was not.'

'On what basis were challenges made?'

'Ask my brief. He ran my defence.'

'Why wasn't Pewley challenged?'

'Probably because we'd run out of challenges by then.'

'Or because he was one of your men?'

'You crazy or something! I'd never set eyes on him before in my life.'

'He used to frequent these parts.'

'If you say so, but I'd never seen him.' He glanced at Big G Ganci and Duke, each of whom shook their heads. 'I swear he'd never been in any of my places.'

'What about your bookshops?'

'How should I know?'

'But you've just sworn he'd never been inside any of your places.'

'Well, he hasn't as far as I know.'

'You want to be careful what you swear, Bernie.'

'Look, Mr Peacock, my life's got enough aggro in it at the moment without your adding to it.'

'Well, round one has cleared the air a bit, I think,' Peacock remarked unconcernedly. 'Now for round two. Do you think Pewley may have been planted on your jury by some unfriendly person?'

'How could he have been?' Mostyn asked slowly in a voice full of suspicion.

'Not easily, I grant you, but it could have been worked.'

'But who?' His tone was still laden with suspicion.

'Someone who would like to see you convicted, Bernie. Someone who'd benefit if you went inside for a spell.'

Mostyn's well nourished features fell into an expression of thoughtfulness. As Nick watched him, he came to realise why he had risen to the top of his particular steaming mound. The features in repose had an unforgiving look. He was a selfish, ruthless man operating in a cut-throat realm.

'Supposing there was such a person,' he said slowly, 'how would he fix someone on my jury?'

Peacock stared at him in surprise. 'Fancy you, Bernie, asking such an innocent question! Anyway, he doesn't have to have been planted. He could have been fixed later. Fixed to make sure you were convicted. Or at least that you weren't acquitted.'

'Yes, he could, couldn't he?' Mostyn said in a tone of dawning satisfaction.

Peacock saw no reason to remind him that majority verdicts had been introduced to frustrate this very thing, let alone that he didn't for one moment think anything of the sort had happened. His purpose was to see how willingly Mostyn bit on the suggestion, as this would be a fair indication of his desire to deflect police attention away from himself.

'You must see, Bernie,' Peacock went on persuasively, 'that Pewley's death was linked with your trial. It's beyond a coincidence that, while serving as a juror in your case, he was murdered by some nut in a North London park. It just doesn't make sense. Surely you see that?'

Mostyn nodded. 'It looks as if it isn't only the police who are giving me aggro.'

'Which of your competitors would gain most if you went inside? Because that's for sure where you'll go when you're convicted.'

'When!' The word came out venomously.

Peacock shrugged. 'You've had a long run, Bernie, but Chief Inspector Scriven's got you by the short and curlies now. Not even an expensive Q.C. is going to save you.'

There were beads of perspiration on Mostyn's forehead and a small vein stood out on his left temple.

'Scriven's bent and I'll prove it.'

'Balls! That's the trouble with you and your sort. You're so bent yourselves that you can't recognise anything that's straight. Anyway, I'm not concerned with that aspect of your affairs. My interest is a dead juror.'

For half a minute, Mostyn remained silent, then suddenly stirring himself, he said, 'I could use another drink.' He glanced round the table and finally at the barman who was reading a newspaper at the farther end. 'Same again, Carlo.'

Nick drowned his whisky from the jug of water on the table. He wondered whether he would ever develop a head like Peacock's. The trouble was you probably couldn't have his head without his liver, too, and by now, that was an organ fit for use in a tanning factory.

'Once this trial's over, I'm getting out,' Mostyn said in a tone verging on self-pity. 'It isn't worth all the aggro.'

'What'll you do?' Peacock enquired with an expression of amused interest.

'I'll go and settle somewhere quietly abroad.'

'The only reason you'll go and settle abroad, Bernie, is because the law's hot on your tail again here and then you'll find yourself extradited.'

'There you go again. I'm sick and tired of being harassed.'

'O.K., O.K.! You're all set for the quiet life, but, meanwhile, you're not helping me much.'

'I don't know how you can say that, Mr Peacock,' Mostyn said in a sorrowful tone.

'Look, Bernie,' Peacock said, leaning forward and staring straight into the other man's face. 'A juror on your case has been murdered, after two others had been threatened. The murdered man was a kinky type who almost certainly used to frequent Soho bookshops and clubs. I have reason to think that he knew a good deal more about you than had ever emerged at your trial.'

'How?'

'I'm not saying for the moment, but that's my firm

belief. And in the light of all that, nothing's going to persuade me that you and his death are not connected.'

'I didn't kill him.'

'But someone else did on your instructions?'

'Never! Anyway, what motive?'

'He was blacking you.'

'How do you work that one out?'

'He was a professional blackmailer.'

Mostyn frowned. 'You mean he had form for blackmail?'

'No, he didn't, but he could have had.'

'How'd he have got on the jury if he had had form?'

'It depends on the person himself claiming disqualification on that ground.'

'Blimey! That's not much of a system, is it? How can I get justice if half the jurors have form?'

'It'd probably increase your chances of acquittal. Birds of a feather et cetera. But I agree that wouldn't be justice from the public's point of view.'

'You twist every bleeding thing,' Mostyn remarked in a tone of disgust.

It was at this moment that a telephone began a muffled ringing somewhere out of sight.

'Take it,' Mostyn said, turning to Ganci.

Ganci got up and went across to a door which was almost invisible in a wall of patterned paper, depicting huge bosomed women in various contortions round an enormous purple couch. As Nick watched, he saw that the handle of the door was the left tit of one of the women. Ganci disappeared through the door which closed behind him. When he emerged, he was frowning and went straight across to whisper in Mostyn's ear.

'Well, tell him, not me,' Mostyn said in a vicious tone.

'It's for you,' Ganci muttered sourly, looking at Nick.

Nick rose from his chair and went over to the door, which, he had noticed, opened outwards. It required quite a pull and one of those pneumatic devices closed it powerfully behind him. He found himself in a small cluttered office. The telephone lay on a cheap, modern desk, mute but expectant.

'Hello,' he said, warily picking up the receiver.

'Nick? This is Clare. Is it all right to speak?'

'Yes, fine. I'm alone.'

'I thought I'd let you know immediately in case it affected what you're doing. There's definitely no reference to Mostyn in any of those cuttings, but there are several to a man named Chirmer, Noel Chirmer, who seems to be one of Soho's emperors.'

'I've heard of him. What do the cuttings say?'

'One relates to his being interviewed by the police about six months ago. It just says he was questioned about a fire at a strip club in Rupert Street but was allowed to go. Chirmer, himself, told the press later that he knew nothing about the fire and was sorry it had happened at the premises of a friend of his.'

'Did he mention the name of the friend?'

'No, but it occurred to me it might be Mostyn.'

'Could be. And for friend read enemy. What are the other bits on Chirmer?'

'It seems he had a girl-friend whose father was a retired colonel and the colonel resented his daughter's friendship with someone he regarded as a Soho mobster. Anyway, the story got into the press when the colonel wrote a blasting sort of letter to one of the Sunday papers, telling all. There's a further cutting indicating that the girl had thrown in her lot with Chirmer, saying he was one of the nicest men she'd ever met and that her father had never understood her.'

'Has a familiar sort of ring! What else?'

'The only other one refers to a Mrs Betsy Chirmer of Leicester whose budgerigar, Rex, had been selected for a T.V. advert.'

'What do you make of that?' he enquired, after a pause.

'Presumably, it was the name Chirmer that caught his eye. It doesn't have any connection with the previous cuttings.'

'Just another example of Flo's industry and thoroughness. What the hell can he have been up to?'

'How are things going your end?'

'I'm not sure. The guvnor's beating about the bush pretty wildly at times.'

'Got anywhere?'

'Not that I can see. I suppose it may add up to something on the basis that the more you get someone to talk, the greater the chance of learning something useful.'

'But Mostyn hasn't made any damaging admissions?'

'Nope.'

'I'd better return to my cuttings. Good-bye, darling.'

''Bye, Clare.'

Nick had been standing beside the desk while talking, letting his gaze range over everything in sight. Towards the end of their conversation, he had pulled open one of the desk drawers. Lying on top of other papers was a list of names, which he had glanced at with little more than idle curiosity. It had then dawned on him that they were familiar names. The names of the twelve jurors in Mostyn's trial. Furthermore, in addition to the twelve names which were typewritten, hand-written addresses appeared beside about eight of them.

For a second, Nick remained undecided whether to remove the list. In the end, he left it where it was, though not without reluctance. It was one of those situations where whatever you did would probably prove to be wrong.

Soon after he rejoined the others, Peacock rose.

'Well, Bernie, I guess that's as far as we can go this evening, but I'll be seeing you again later.'

'Look, Mr Peacock,' Mostyn said in an ill-fitting tone of sincerity, 'I wouldn't try and fool you. You have my word that I know nothing about this juror's death. To me, the jury were no more than twelve faceless men, who held my fate in their hands. Despite what I said earlier, I believe in the jury system and in British justice. I not only believe in it, I respect it and I can't say fairer than that – especially after all the aggro I've had.'

Peacock received this tribute to the country's trial system with a sardonic smile. Then turning on his heel, he hurried up the stairs with Nick behind him. A few yards down the street, he led the way into a coffee bar.

'What was your call?' he asked when they were sitting at a small table with two cups of Espresso coffee in front of them. Nick told him and he said, 'Chirmer, eh? I wonder if he's friend or foe. We'll ask Scriven.' When Nick went on to mention the list of jurors' names and addresses he'd found in the desk drawer, Peacock said grimly, 'So they were no more than twelve faceless men to him, were they! Pity you didn't seize the list. On the other hand, maybe it's better you didn't. By leaving it there, they won't have been put on guard.' He sipped his scalding coffee and made a face. 'Don't know how anyone can drink this muck,' he observed, adding three further spoonfuls of sugar to his cup. In a more reflective tone, he went on, 'We've got the last six hours of Flo's life to account for. From the time he left the office in Eve Place to the time he met his death in Jessamyn Park. Someone must have seen him somewhere during that period. One presumes he was on his way home when he was murdered, so where had he been spending the evening? Where?'

'We'd better organise house to house enquiries in the vicinity of Jessamyn Park without further delay, sir.'

Peacock nodded. 'Also at pubs in the area and at the nearest bus stops and underground station. But before we do that, we must have some photos of him.' Nick braced himself for what was coming. 'I want him photographed in each of his wigs and sets made up. They can be sort of candid camera shots.'

'They won't show much variety of expression,' Nick observed, with a shudder.

'Never mind his expression.'

'What about his eyes? People won't like looking at photos of an obviously dead man. There'll be complaints.'

'I saw a pair of dark glasses in his flat. Put those on him, then no one'll see whether he's alive or dead.'

'Very well, sir,' Nick said without enthusiasm.

'No good being squeamish in this job,' Peacock observed, grimacing as he took another sip of coffee.

It was as they were leaving the coffee shop that Nick put a restraining hand on Peacock's arm.

'What's up?'

'That man who's just gone by on the other side of the road, sir. I recognised him. It's Fielden, the foreman of Mostyn's jury.'

CHAPTER NINE

After several minutes' observation, Nick began to wonder if Fielden was anything more than an ordinary Soho visitor.

He walked slowly, glancing about him all the while and, from time to time, studying the window displays of shops whose simple designation was 'Books and Magazines'. Twice he entered such establishments, but didn't stay long in either. Eventually, he reached Shaftesbury Avenue and joined a bus queue.

As Nick retraced his steps to where he had left Peacock, he reviewed in his mind just what Fielden's activities had amounted to. He had shown an obvious interest in all the porn shops and an equal interest in the various forms of sleazy entertainment on offer. On the other hand, he had shown no interest at all in any of the numerous restaurants or of the occasional more staid forms of business enterprise.

If his jury had still been in being, one could have assumed that he was making his own first-hand assessment of the background against which Mostyn's activities had to be judged. But this was no longer the case, so what was he doing prowling about Soho in a semi-aimless fashion? He hadn't been in search of a meal and he hadn't made any purchases and he hadn't dived through any of the ill-lit doorways leading to the more expensive, and often fraudulent, forms of entertainment.

Peacock's only reaction when told all this was to grunt and add that it was something to store away in their minds.

It was about nine o'clock by the time they got back to headquarters and there was a message asking them to ring a Mr Brundle as soon as they came in.

'And who is this Brundle?' Peacock enquired without enthusiasm.

'I understood he's the dead man's solicitor, sir,' Clare replied.

'Works late, doesn't he?'

'He was phoning from home. He'd been away and only learnt of his client's death when he returned late this afternoon.'

'Where's home?'

'Canonbury.'

'Oh! Well, you call him, Nick, and find out what he wants to tell us.'

Before doing so, Nick went in search of a Law List. He decided he would like to form an idea of Mr Brundle's standing, and that of his firm, before speaking to him.

'Edwin Brundle,' he read, 'admitted May 1958.' His firm was E. Brundle & Co., of which Edwin appeared to be the partnerless principal. Its place of business was in the King's Cross Road.

Armed with these details, Nick put through the call.

The phone at the other end was answered promptly.

'Mr Brundle?'

'Mr Brundle speaking,' replied a rather high-pitched voice.

'I'm Detective Sergeant Attwell. I gather you phoned about Mr Pewley's death.'

'Indeed I did, at the first opportunity. I'm still reeling from the shock of it. I'd been staying in the wilds of Lincolnshire for a few days and I never see any newspapers when I'm there. It's my sister's place. She lives in the depths of the Wolds. And so it wasn't until I reached my office late this afternoon that I learnt the dreadful news.' As though further explanation was needed, he added, 'She's not on the telephone either, which is not as extraordinary as it sounds, seeing that she's stone deaf. Dates from when she had measles very badly as an adolescent.'

'Mr Pewley was your client, I gather?' Nick cut in before Mr Brundle could embark on a further run of family reminiscence.

'He was more than a client, Sergeant. He was a friend of many years standing. A cherished friend.'

With quickened interest, Nick said, 'Would you like us to come and see you this evening?'

'I think that would be a most desirable course, Sergeant. If you have a pencil and a piece of paper handy, I'll give you my address.'

Peacock was busy organising further lines of enquiry when Nick reported to him.

'Well, it'll help to shed more light on Flo,' he said. 'And don't forget to ask him if there's a will.' He paused. 'If you hadn't gathered, I'm not coming with you!'

'From the sound of him on the phone, I picture Mr Brundle as looking a bit like Flo,' Nick remarked.

Peacock's only reaction was to assume an expression of distaste and give Nick a dismissing wave.

Mr Brundle occupied the ground-floor flat of a converted Victorian house in a crescent of similar houses. His front door opened off the main hall of the house which had a musty smell befitting its appearance.

The door opened to reveal a small, dapper man wearing a chunky cardigan which reached almost to his knees. A pair of green corduroy trousers gave the appearance of starting where the cardigan stopped. He had one of those unnaturally young faces and a head of carefully tended golden hair.

'Oh do come in, Sergeant,' he said, at the same time shaking Nick's hand.

He led the way into a large, high-ceilinged room which, as Nick was later to tell Clare, resembled a museum with its cabinets of china and glass-topped tables of trinkets. The sofa and chairs were also Victorian pieces complete with embroided antimacassars. Nick half expected to find the room lit by gas. Even so, the two electric standard lamps had pink silk shades, each with a fringe.

'I hope you don't mind cats,' Mr Brundle remarked as Nick was glancing about him.

It was then he noticed an enormous black cat curled up asleep on one of the chairs. He shook his head.

'Then if you sit over there, we needn't disturb Justinian. I always have to explain to my non-legal friends who Justinian was, but I'm sure you know?'

'A Roman emperor, wasn't he?'

'Yes and a notable law reformer, too.' Mr Brundle stood hesitantly beside the sofa. 'Now, before we start talking business, can I offer you a little refreshment. A glass of wine, perhaps?'

'No, I won't have anything, thank you, Mr Brundle.'

'Very well.' Mr Brundle sat down on the edge of the sofa. 'I think I'd better tell you all I can first and leave you to ask me questions afterwards. That'll probably be the most satisfactory way of conducting our business.' He clasped his hands on his lap. 'Laurence Pewley was not only a client, but a friend. I first met him about three years ago when I had professional dealings with his firm. We soon discovered that we had a number of common interests and shortly afterwards he asked me if I'd be his solicitor, a proposition to which I gladly assented.' Mr Brundle gazed fondly at his cat. 'He was a lonely sort of person and I like to think that he valued my companionship.'

'How often used you to see him?' Nick broke in.

'Not all that frequently, but we used to talk together on the telephone once a fortnight or so.'

'Did you ever visit his home?'

'Never. He used to say that after seeing mine, he wouldn't wish me to visit his. I suppose he felt it might inhibit our relationship and I respected his feelings.' He gave Nick a sad look. 'There is quite a contrast, I expect?'

Nick, who wouldn't have wanted to live in either of their places, contented himself with a nod. Mr Brundle was about to resume his narrative when Nick interrupted him again.

'Who is his next of kin?'

'He had no family at all. He was an only child born to elderly parents who died many years ago. He once told me he had a distant cousin in New Zealand, but he'd never met her, nor did they ever correspond. And she was the only relative he was aware of.'

'Did he leave a will?'

'He did, indeed, thanks to my insistence. He took a lot of persuading, but eventually he made one.'

'Who benefits under it?'

'A cats' home.'

'But he didn't own a cat!'

'He'd grown very fond of Justinian,' Mr Brundle said primly. 'What happened was that when I kept on telling him it was criminal foolishness not to make a will as the State was the least deserving beneficiary anyone could think of, he said he'd like to leave everything he had to me. I told him I couldn't possibly accept such a proposal in the circumstances and I suggested he should make a will in favour of charity. At first, he said he didn't have any favourite charities, but, later, he quite suddenly told me one day that he'd decided to leave everything to a cats' home as a gesture to Justinian and the nation's great family of cats.'

'Which particular cats' home did he choose?' Nick asked in an awed voice.

'The St Francis Group of Homes.'

'How much will his estate be worth?'

'Not a great deal. He had between two and three thousand pounds in savings and, apart from that, it's just the contents of his home.'

'He didn't own it?'

'No, it was leasehold.'

Realising that Mr Brundle appeared to have accepted his seizure of the initiative, Nick quickly mustered his thoughts on the further matters he wanted to probe.

'I suppose you knew he was sitting on an Old Bailey jury at the time of his death?'

'Yes, indeed, and I was very glad for him, as I'd often felt he didn't have sufficient outlets for his wide interest in the world around us.'

'Had you seen him since he'd been on the jury?'

'He called in here on his way home the second or third day of the trial.'

'Did he make any comments on it?'

'On the trial, you mean?' Mr Brundle enquired in his precise tone.

'Yes.'

'He was clearly finding it a most interesting and rewarding experience.'

'Rewarding?'

Mr Brundle frowned. 'Intellectually rewarding,' he said, tartly. 'I don't know what else you thought I meant.'

'Did he tell you about the case?'

'Yes.'

'The porn side of it wasn't upsetting him?'

'He gave me no such impression.'

'Did he say anything about the accused?'

'Nothing that I recall.'

'Did he mention that some members of the jury had been the subject of intimidation?'

'Yes, he did tell me that.'

'Did he appear to have any worries on that score himself?'

'He said he wondered who'd be next, if there was a next.'

'But did he mention any intimidation directed at himself?'

'Certainly not. If he had done, I should have advised him to let the police know at once.' Mr Brundle unclasped and then reclasped his hands. 'Do I take it from your line of questioning, Sergeant, you're working on the theory that he was murdered as a direct consequence of his jury service?'

'It's a possibility we can't overlook.'

The solicitor shook his head sadly. 'Poor, poor Laurence! The terrible irony of it! There he was performing a high civic duty with far more zeal than most people show when summoned for jury service and it ends in his death. I can't get over the tragedy.' He continued slowly shaking his head until finally he brought his gaze to rest on Nick. 'Do you know that this is the first time one of my clients has ever been murdered?'

Nick registered a hint of Gallic resignation. He wasn't at all sure how he was expected to react to this somewhat curious piece of rhetoric. It was as if Mr Brundle had observed that it was the first time one of his cats had ever been run over.

'Did you know about his press cuttings?' he asked, after a pause.

'He told me he was always cutting out items from

newspapers and sticking them into scrapbooks.'

'Had he told you what sort of items they were?'

'I gathered they were articles, critiques, things of that sort.'

'We've not found anything like that. The books we've come across are full of much more personal material, mostly concerning people's peccadilloes.'

'He had a profound interest in the human plight,' Mr Brundle said loftily.

'What we found was the sort of material a potential blackmailer might have kept,' Nick retorted.

Mr Brundle's reaction to this was so sharp that Justinian woke up.

'I assure you, Sergeant, that my late client was no blackmailer. It's an utterly preposterous idea.'

'Nevertheless, you weren't aware that he collected cuttings of that nature?'

'Not of that precise nature, no,' Mr Brundle conceded grudgingly. 'I hope, Sergeant,' he went on in a lecturing tone, 'that you are not one of those officers who jumps to unwarranted conclusions when confronted by the unorthodox in life. It is possible to keep press cuttings without being a blackmailer, to give sweets to strange children without being a pederast or to read the Marquis de Sade without being a dangerous pervert. All too often these days someone who doesn't fit into one of the standard moulds is viewed with suspicion by the middle-class masses. Witch hunts are never far from the common mind, I regret to say.'

'I promise you I haven't jumped to any conclusions about Mr Pewley. I was merely stating a fact and drawing a possible inference. I never said he *was* a blackmailer and, indeed, there's no proof that he was one. However, knowing him as you did, perhaps *you* can suggest what his interest would have been in collecting the type of personal material I've described?'

Mr Brundle assumed the faintly put-upon expression

of one always being asked to do other people's work.

'He had this remarkable memory, you know. It occurred to me more than once that he used to store away an enormous amount of trivia in it, though, naturally, I never suggested anything of the sort to him. But, for example, if you happened to say to him that you'd read in the paper about the president of the Butterfly Collectors' Society being knocked down by a bus in Piccadilly, he'd immediately be able to tell you everything else that had ever been printed about the unfortunate man. That's rather a far-fetched example, but he did have this phenomenal facility for total recollection.'

'People at his firm were telling us about it,' Nick put in.

'Of course, a memory such as his harnessed to a job made him a most valuable employee.' Focusing Nick with a judicial gaze, Mr Brundle went on, 'I suggest that, until you have any evidence to the contrary – and I very much doubt whether any will be forthcoming – you regard his scrapbooks of cuttings as nothing more than the fruits of a hobby. An unusual hobby, maybe, but a perfectly harmless one.'

Nick received the advice without comment. 'Did you know he wore a wig?' he asked suddenly.

'I did. Quite a lot of people do, you know!' As he spoke, Nick found himself glancing irresistibly at the solicitor's thatch of golden hair. 'I am *not* referring to myself,' Mr Brundle remarked crossly. 'Laurence had several wigs and used to wear different ones for different occasions. And why not?'

'No reason at all,' Nick said defensively in the face of Mr Brundle's suddenly aggressive tone. 'Though it is rather unusual.'

'Unusual! Good heavens, can't one be unusual, as you put it, without exciting stupid suspicion! I happen to sleep in a sarong, which is unusual for a resident of Canonbury. I eat marmalade with mackerel which, I imagine, is unusual anywhere. I do beg of you, Sergeant, not to be hidebound by so-called accepted convention.'

'I don't consider I am,' Nick said, stung by the accusation of being a conventionally mindless policeman.

'Good! Good!' Mr Brundle said keenly as though he had just exorcised an evil spirit. 'And now there's something else we must discuss, namely, poor Laurence's funeral arrangements. I take it I can go ahead and make these?'

'It'll be, of course, for the coroner to release the body for burial,' Nick said cautiously.

'I'm aware of that. But provided the police don't object, I'm sure he won't.'

'I don't think the police'll have any objections. There's been a P.M. and it's not a case in which there can be any dispute as to cause of death, so there's no need to keep the body.'

Mr Brundle gave a refined shudder. 'I'm relieved to hear that. This pagan business of retaining bodies in mortuary refrigerators for weeks, even months, after death has always seemed to me an affront to one's Christian susceptibilities.'

'Sometimes it's necessary.'

'So it is claimed,' Mr Brundle replied disdainfully.

'Did he leave any burial wishes?'

'Apart from the fact that he wished to be interred and not cremated, none.'

Nick thought it better not to comment that this would suit the police better, anyway, as he could always be dug up again if necessary.

A few minutes later, Nick made as if to get up and Mr Brundle sprang agilely to his feet. Justinian was fast asleep again, his well-fed black bulk occupying the whole chair.

'I'm so glad we've met,' Mr Brundle said as he led the way towards the front door. 'And I have no doubt that we shall be in further touch with each other shortly. I'll let you know as soon as I've made the funeral arrangements and I shall want from you the keys to Laurence's flat. An inventory will have to be taken for estate duty purposes.' He shook his head sadly again. 'Poor, poor Laurence, a person of gentle goodness if ever there were!'

It had been a long, but interesting, day, Nick reflected as he drove back to headquarters. Gathering information about the murdered man had been like collecting the skins shed by a chameleon. Poor Laurence or baleful Flo? Which was he?

CHAPTER TEN

Clare was still at work when he returned. In front of her was a large sheet of paper ruled in columns with Flo's volumes of press cuttings stacked to her right.

'How are you getting on?' Nick asked.

'It'll take longer than I thought,' she said, with a sigh.

'His solicitor thinks he did it only as a hobby.'

To his surprise, Clare didn't immediately dismiss the idea. 'They're such a curious mixture,' she said, 'I suppose some of them might be fodder for a blackmailer, but others couldn't possibly be. And even the ones that could be put to blackmailing use ... well, the very existence of a newspaper cutting removes the normal blackmailer's lever, namely threat of disclosure.'

'So what conclusion have you drawn?'

'I haven't. But the solicitor could be right. His hobby was collecting cuttings about people's peccadilloes.' When Nick looked sceptical, she reached for one of the files and opened it. 'All right, listen to this one then. "Thirty-two-year-old milkman, Leslie Woods of Leather Place, Wimbledon, had his face slapped by attractive blonde Mrs Yvonne Johns, 21-year-old mother of two, when he tried to force his way into her kitchen. Mr Woods said later that it was all a misunderstanding and that he was only trying to be helpful. 'She had her hands full with her kiddies,' he said, 'and I only came into the kitchen to put her yoghurt on the table.' He denied making any sort of comment which could have justified the slap. 'I expect she was feeling a bit nervy,' he said, 'but I don't intend to let it bother me and I don't bear her any grudge. I shall still help the ladies I deliver to when I can. Most of them appreciate it.' Mrs Johns said the matter was now closed as far as she was concerned. She wished now, she said, that she hadn't ever mentioned it to her neighbour, Mrs Jackson."' Clare looked up. 'Now, what possible interest could he have had in cutting that out of the paper and pasting it into a book?'

'Are there any other references on the card to this helpful milkman?'

'Yes, there's another cutting two years ago relating to a court appearance. He was fined £5 for indecent exposure.'

'Well, that puts a rather different complexion on it.'

'In what way?'

'It looks as if he may have been up to the same thing again. That's why he got his face slapped.'

'O.K., but what interest is that to Flo?'

'I agree, it's difficult to see why he should have taken the trouble to cut it out of a newspaper.' He pursed his lips. 'One way of finding out would be to tackle things from the other end.'

'Exactly,' Clare said, with a gratified smile.

'You'd already thought of that?'

'Not only thought of it, but got Peacock's blessing to enquiring along that line.'

Nick frowned. 'On your own?'

'On my own,' she said in a pleased voice. 'It's a job made for a resourceful young woman detective constable.' She laughed as she observed Nick's worried expression. 'Don't look so anxious, darling. You forget I learnt judo at training school.'

'But you've never had occasion to practise it.'

'I'm sure it'll be good enough to fend off any flashing milkman.'

'Who are you going to call on?'

'I'll select about four to start with and see where that gets me. I'll choose the most recent cuttings where there's a prospect of tracing the person referred to.'

'I don't want you nosing round Soho on your own.'

'I shan't.'

'Nor visiting any real criminals.'

'I shan't do that either, assuming you don't regard milkman Woods as a real criminal.' She grinned. 'I'd have thought he was only a mini-criminal by anyone's standards.'

'I don't regard any sex offenders as mini,' he said grimly.

Clare laughed. 'I may be your fiancée, darling, but I am still a police officer. Anyway, I shall be both careful and discreet. All I want to find out is whether Flo has been in touch with any of the people I visit. And if he has, what was the nature of his business?'

'It will certainly help to know that,' he said emphatically. 'Have you already decided whom you're going to interview?'

Clare nodded. 'Mr Woods, the milkman for a start. And then there's a Roy King, who is a pop group manager and who lives in Chelsea. He's twice been the subject of paternity proceedings which have been widely reported in Sunday papers.' She glanced at a piece of paper on top of one of the files. 'I thought I might try Gordon Arthur Baker, though I doubt whether I'll get very far with him.'

'I remember his name from my quick riffle through,' Nick said. 'Wasn't he an absconding cashier?'

'That's right.'

'But that was years ago.'

'Five to be exact. But there's another cutting only two months old saying the police had been to an address in West London, but had not found him.'

'And what makes you think you will?'

'Nothing, but I'm intrigued at this further mention five years after the first. There'll be someone at the address even if it's not Gordon Arthur Baker.'

'And?'

'My last name for the moment is Fritz Cantor who lives at Uxbridge and whose warehouse was mysteriously burnt down a few months ago.'

'Is that all about Mr Cantor?'

Clare nodded. 'He hasn't figured in the Pewley book of records before or since.'

A sudden thought seemed to strike Nick. 'Do any of the cuttings refer to women?'

'None that I've come across as yet.' Clare cocked her head on one side. 'And what does that say to you, Sergeant?'

'That he found them a less interesting subject of study than the stronger sex,' Nick replied with a grin. He glanced at his watch. 'Why don't we call it a day? The guvnor's packed it up till tomorrow. It's time we did the same.'

Clare nodded. 'I'll leave the rest of these till the morning.' As she spoke, she gathered up the volumes of cuttings and carried them across to a cupboard.

'I'll drive you home,' Nick said, though the offer scarcely needed to be made in the circumstances.

'Perhaps I can persuade you to drop in for a cup of cocoa,' Clare replied lifting her coat from a hanger behind the door. 'There's nothing like cocoa for cementing cordial relations between ranks.'

Nick enveloped her with an arm and squeezed her to his side. 'I hope you'll be as thoughtful when we're married.'

CHAPTER ELEVEN

It was one of those vast, depressing cemeteries that London had allowed to spread, like an ugly rash, on her face. At first glance, one wouldn't have thought a vacant plot existed midst the acres of unsightly marble headstones, each of them marking with some pious cliché the passing of a 'loved one'.

Nick who regarded himself as only a mildly religious person could actually feel his spirituality shrinking into a small lump within him.

The grey day did nothing to elevate his spirit, nor, from their appearance, the spirits of those standing around Flo's grave. The dreary service of commitment, with its language of doom, was, at last, coming to an end. Soon the mourners would file along the neat criss-cross paths on their way out of the cemetery, leaving Flo alone in his slit in the ground waiting to be covered over by the sexton's men.

Nick, who had been deputed to attend the funeral, had half-expected to find himself and Mr Brundle the only two there. He had therefore been surprised when Vic Fielden arrived with seven other jurors. As they left the cemetery chapel after the first part of the service, Vic and his jurors had posed for a press photograph, in which Vic had stood in the centre like the captain of a football team. They were all wearing black ties and assumed expressions of solemn decorum for the benefit of the photographer.

Nick had fallen into step beside Vic Fielden as they followed the coffin's winding route to its place of burial.

'I call it very nice of you all to come to the funeral,' he said.

'It was everyone's wish to do so,' Fielden said with a touch of pride. 'Three couldn't take time off to attend, but only one made it clear that he wasn't going to come.'

'Who was that?' Nick asked, glancing round at those who were following them.

'Mr Brigstock.'

Nick had, in fact, noticed Mr Brigstock's absence, which had not surprised him. He was rather more surprised to find that Mr White *had* turned up, after the impression he had gained of him during the Old Bailey interview.

'I was hoping you might have made an arrest by now,' Fielden went on.

'It's only three days since the discovery of the murder,' Nick protested.

'We all realise that, but so long as the murderer is at large, we're bound to feel uneasy.'

'You mean all of you on the Mostyn jury?'

'Yes.'

'I don't quite see why, as you're no longer trying the case.'

'That hasn't necessarily removed the danger.'

'Can you explain what you mean?' Nick said, with a puzzled frown, temporarily forgetting the precariously borne coffin ahead and the incongruous surroundings.

'Until you find out the precise motive for Laurence's death, any one of us could be struck down for the same reason.'

'But what reason?'

'Because we could be in possession of knowledge dangerous to the murderer. Without knowing it, that is.'

'But if you don't know it, how can it be dangerous knowledge?'

'Because something might happen, which would suddenly make us a danger to him. That's what must have happened in Laurence's case.'

'You make it sound as if you're all going around like

time bombs,' Nick blurted out.

'I hardly think this is an occasion for jokes,' Fielden said severely.

'It wasn't intended as a joke, but I really don't think any of you are in danger now the trial has been stopped.' Nick realised, however, that it probably suited Vic Fielden's ego to consider himself as being in some danger and, accordingly, nothing Nick was likely to say would dissolve the feeling. 'Have you yourself had any further thoughts as to who the murderer could be?' he asked quickly as they were approaching the graveside.

'I've no doubt it was someone connected with Mostyn. I thought that was the police view, too.'

'You haven't discovered anything yourself?'

Fielden gave him a sharp sidelong glance, before shaking his head as though perplexed by the question.

The priest stood at the head of the grave with Mr Brundle nearest to him. Nick moved to a position beside Mr White while Davey, Weir, Berenger and the others shuffled themselves into the limited space round the grave.

'Man that is born of a woman hath but a short time to live and is full of misery,' the priest intoned. 'He cometh up and is cut down, like a flower ...'

Nick felt his mind congealing. Flo had been cut down all right, rather more dramatically than the words normally envisaged. He decided to switch off and not listen. He glanced at the still forms around him.

As a solicitor, Mr Brundle probably attended more funerals than most. At all events, he certainly gave the appearance of being more at home than the rest of them, with his expression of graven attention. Next to him, Vic Fielden had the air of someone out to win an award as mourner of the year. His 'amens' were louder than anyone else's and his head was bowed in an attitude of exaggerated reverence. On his other side was Ian Berenger who fidgeted most of the time and smiled whenever he caught anyone's eye. Philip Weir and David Davey each looked cold and anxious and Nick guessed that it would not have occurred to either of them to attend had not Vic Fielden leant on them. There were three others whose names Nick was unsure of and whose expressions were a mixture of dutiful and bored. And lastly there was Mr White.

In his own way, Mr White looked as at home as Mr Brundle. He stood quietly without any assumed attitude, his silvery hair riffled by the chilly breeze, his eyes fixed on the coffin in a faraway expression.

'I didn't expect to see you here,' Nick said to him, as the service ended and they turned away from the grave-side.

'I'd been given the impression by Fielden that it was going to be a hundred per cent turnout,' Mr White said with a thin smile. 'Though I wasn't surprised not to see Mr Brigstock here. Anyway, as I was able to get away from my office, I thought I'd attend. Apart from paying last respects to a recent colleague, I reckoned it would give one an opportunity of finding out how police enquiries were going.' He paused, gave a small frown and added, 'Not that I was really expecting to see you here, Sergeant. What I meant was that it would provide an opportunity for us to swap news between ourselves.' Observing Nick's expression, he added, 'Oh, perhaps you didn't know, Fielden has arranged for us to have lunch together at a nearby pub.'

'No, I didn't know that.'

'Well, if you want to talk to any of us, there's your chance.' He turned his head to look at Nick. 'How *are* your enquiries going?'

'We're still in the sifting stage.'

'No clues?'

'Oh, lots of clues. One might say too many clues.'

'But no prospect of an early arrest?'

'Oh, I wouldn't rule that out either.'

Mr White gave a slight shrug, as though to indicate he could recognise a stone wall when he saw one.

'My turn to ask you a question,' Nick said in a disarming tone. 'Have you any worries for your own safety now the trial has been abandoned?'

'No-o, I don't think so,' Mr White said slowly. 'I didn't really have any before.'

'I gather some of the jurors did have and, possibly, still have.'

'I suppose it depends on whether one relates the intimidation of Weir and Davey to the murder of Pewley.'

'And you don't?'

'Yes and no. Yes, in that I feel Mostyn was responsible for all three incidents. No, in that I don't believe Pewley's death was an act of intimidation of the rest of us.'

'You think he was murdered for some reason peculiar to himself?'

'Yes.'

'What?'

'I haven't an idea. It's simply that the other theory doesn't make sense. Well, does it?'

'Only if murder wasn't actually intended. If the attacker only wanted to do him an injury and scare the wits out of him, it would fit with the intimidation theory.'

'You know more about these things than I, but, if that was the intention, surely a different method would have been used. Beating up is the most obvious way to effect that sort of purpose.'

'Perhaps,' Nick said, non-committally. They had reached the stone gate-house which stood at the entrance to the cemetery and paused. 'There is one other question I should ask you. When you parted company with Pewley that last evening after court, did he say anything about bread?'

'Bread?' Mr White echoed in surprise.

'Yes.'

'No, nothing at all. Why on earth should he have mentioned bread?'

'Because that's what he said to a colleague when he arrived at his firm later.'

'What? That he was going to buy bread?'

'No, not actually buy it. The person concerned merely got the impression that bread figured in some way in his evening's arrangements.'

Mr White frowned heavily and shook his head. 'Sounds extraordinary! But he certainly never said anything about bread to me before we parted company.' He was thoughtful for a moment. 'It's not for me to make suggestions, but is it possible he was using the word in a colloquial sense?'

'Very possible.'

At that moment, Mr Brundle came hurrying up. 'Ah! I was hoping to catch you before you left, Sergeant. If you remember, you said you'd let me have the key to Laurence's flat. Now that the funeral is over, I must make a start on his estate.'

'We don't have the key, I'm afraid.'

'But surely it was in one of his pockets?'

'Since speaking to you the other evening, I've personally checked through everything that was found on him and there's no door key. The only keys were on a ring. Three small ones which opened cupboards.'

'But that's very curious! This was a key with a bit of yellow tape tied at the end.'

'We've never found such a key.'

'Well, where on earth is it?' Mr Brundle asked imperiously.

'I've no idea. But may I ask how you're able to describe it?'

'What on earth do you mean?' he demanded in a tone which had become a shade shrill.

'When we talked the other evening, you said you've never set foot inside his home, so I'm just wondering how you know what his front-door key looked like?'

'Really, Sergeant! Are you telling me I'm under suspicion?'

'No, but I'd still be interested to have an answer to my question.'

'I happen to know because once or twice when he was searching his pocket for something or other, he fetched out his door key and on one occasion he drew attention to its yellow ribbon. I hope that satisfies you?'

Nick nodded. He had no intention of grovelling and, moreover, intended to check with others who might have seen the yellow-ribboned key. But, for the moment, it was its disappearance which was puzzling him. When police had arrived at the flat, the front door had been locked, so presumably Flo had taken the key with him when he left on his final errand. And yet it wasn't in his possession when his body was found. So what inference did one draw from that?'

'I regard the disappearance of his door key as most significant,' Mr Brundle said, breaking in on his thoughts. 'I hope it's something the police will follow up immediately.'

'Of course.'

'Meanwhile, I'll have to get a locksmith to let me into the flat.' He paused a moment before adding, 'It looks to me very much as if the murderer took the key after killing Laurence.' This being Nick's own line of thought, he nodded. 'As to why is a matter for surmise,' Mr Brundle went on, 'though there does seem one obvious inference. Namely, that the murderer wished to return to the flat for some purpose. Did you find any evidence of disturbance when you gained entry?'

'No.'

'Well, I can see I've given you some food for thought,' the solicitor remarked in a tone of satisfaction. 'And now I must be getting back to my office.'

Nick found himself alone as Mr Brundle walked across

to the hired car waiting on the other side of the road. Bet that's being paid for out of Flo's assets, he reflected wryly, as he watched Mr Brundle settle himself into the back.

A verger, whom Nick had noticed in the cemetery chapel, was coming down the path towards him.

'Looks like we're going to have rain,' he remarked as he reached Nick.

'I wouldn't be surprised,' Nick replied, rather as one making a conventional move in a game of draughts. 'I gathered the other mourners at Mr Pewley's funeral were off to lunch at a pub in the vicinity. Would you happen to know which it is?'

'The Queen of Hearts. It's in the High Street about half a mile from here.'

'Thanks. I think I know it.'

He wasn't yet sure whether he intended breaking in on the party, but he'd go along and have a sandwich and a pint and decide his next move then.

CHAPTER TWELVE

As events turned out, the decision was made for him.

The pub was full of lunchtime customers and Nick had wedged himself into a corner of the saloon bar. He was half-way through a pint of bitter and was munching a cold roast beef sandwich, idly reflecting that the best sandwiches were still to be found in pubs, when he felt a tap on the shoulder. He turned to see the beaming face of Ian Berenger.

'Hello,' Berenger said. 'Why don't you come and join us? Vic's laid on a private room upstairs. It's quite a reunion.'

'I've not been invited,' Nick said in a doubtful tone.

'I'm inviting you now.'

'All right.'

'Well, hang on while I go off to the gents. I'll be back in a second.'

Nick had finished his own meal by the time Berenger reappeared and accompanied him to the room upstairs where Vic Fielden and the others were standing around in not very animated groups.

'Look who I found downstairs,' Berenger called out as he and Nick entered the room.

Nick could not but notice that the atmosphere became, if anything, less animated at this announcement and that Vic Fielden's own expression was far from welcoming.

'Oh, hello!' he said in a distinctly cool tone. 'We're buying our own drinks,' he added pointedly, indicating a small bar on the far side of the room.

'Let me get you something,' Mr White said with an air of faint amusement as he stepped forward. 'I'm drinking whisky. Same for you?'

'Thanks, but I'd sooner have a glass of beer.' He followed Mr White over to the bar. 'My arrival seemed to put a bit of a dampener on the party.'

'I think Fielden was about to voice a few criticisms of the police handling of the case. I presume he won't wish to do so as long as you're here.'

'In that case, I'd better drink up and get out. What is he especially critical of?'

'Mainly that you've not seen fit to provide us with any protection since the trial.'

'Well, you're all still alive, aren't you?' Nick said in an abrasive tone.

'So far.'

'If we believed any of you were in danger as a result of what's happened, we'd obviously do something about it. But we don't and events have proved us right.'

'So far.'

'It almost sounds as if you're on his side now over this.'

'No,' Mr White said mildly, 'I'm somewhere in the middle.'

'Well, please tell Mr Fielden and the rest of them what I've said.'

'Why not stay and tell them yourself?'

'All right, I will,' Nick said, and walked across to where Fielden was talking with Davey and Berenger. 'I wonder if I could say something on behalf of the police while you're all here together,' he said, addressing the ex-foreman of the jury.

Fielden said nothing for several seconds, then turning round he clapped his hands for silence and said, 'The sergeant here would like to say a few words.'

'It's just this, gentlemen,' Nick said, raising his voice. 'Police enquiries are continuing as vigorously as possible and our file won't be closed until we've made an arrest and have a convicted murderer tucked up in prison. From our enquiries to date, we are satisfied that none of you stand in any personal danger as a result of the murder. Should we have reason to think otherwise, we shall immediately take the necessary steps.'

'It may be a bit late by then,' Fielden observed, glancing at the others for support.

The general reaction was to stare at Nick as cows stare at a stranger in their field. Only the weak-chinned Philip Weir cast an uncomfortable look at the floor, leaving Nick to wonder for what reason.

'Have any of you received any hint of a threat, any suggestion of unpleasantness, since the trial ended?' he asked robustly.

There was a mixture of murmured 'no's' and shaken heads, with only Weir continuing to gaze distractedly at his feet.

'Mr Weir?' Nick said. 'You've not been intimidated further, have you?'

Weir appeared to raise his eyes reluctantly from the floor, only to return his gaze there after a quick shake of his head.

'Well, there you are!' he said to Fielden. 'I really am sure you have nothing to worry about on that score. But if any of you do have cause to suspect otherwise, get in touch with us immediately. And if anyone has any further information to give, please also let us know at once. Sometimes one recalls things only later.' He looked round him with an expectant expression, but no one made a move or said anything. Feeling increasingly like a gate-crasher, Nick downed his beer and made to leave. He cast a final glance in the direction of Philip Weir whose air of unease was still manifest. Though he affected to be listening to Berenger, who was talking to him, it was plain that his mind was elsewhere.

At the bottom of the stairs, Nick paused and looked back. He wondered whether Weir might follow him down to speak to him privately, but no one came and Nick left.

About the same time as he was driving away from the Queen of Hearts, Les Duke was returning to the Petronella Club. He used his own key to enter and ran down the stairs with the agility of one who could identify each step in the dark. A single naked bulb lit the deserted basement club and Duke, moving with the assurance of a cat, made for the door of Mostyn's office. He knocked on it softly and called out, 'It's me, Les.'

The door was opened by Ganci who stood back to let him enter. Bernie Mostyn was leaning back in his chair with his feet on the desk. He had a glass in his hand.

'I'm back,' Les Duke said in a pleased tone.

'So we can see! Get yourself a drink and come to the point.'

Duke went across to the small, lit wall cupboard which was already open to reveal a well-stocked bar. He poured himself a whisky and sat down.

'Well, I saw him all right,' he announced in the same pleased voice.

'Did he see you? That's the point!'

'Yes and it really gave him the frighteners.'

'Look, Les,' Mostyn said in an exasperated voice, 'we're not kids listening to a bloody serial. We want the whole story now, not in bloody instalments.'

'O.K., Bernie, I'm trying to tell you, but you keep interrupting.'

Mostyn thrust his glass at Ganci.

'For Chrissake get me another drink before this boy makes me do my nut. He's worse than some of those legal types who never come to the point.'

Duke grinned, but in a somewhat tentative fashion.

'I parked the car just opposite the cemetery entrance,' he said quickly before Mostyn could start grumbling again. 'I got there early so I could see 'em all arrive. Weir was one of the last. He was on his own and just as he was about to turn in through the gate, I gave him a bit of a whistle. When he saw me, he looked real scared.'

'So he recognised you all right?'

'He certainly did.'

'Good! Go on.'

'Well, I just gave him a good old stare and when he continued acting like a hypnotised rabbit, I just said all nice like, "Hadn't you better hurry, Mr Weir, or you'll be late?" and he turned and scuttled into the cemetery. I then scouted around and found he'd parked his car in a side street about two hundred yards away, so I drove mine round and parked behind it. When he returned, he had one of the others with him whom he was giving a lift, so I couldn't speak to him, but he saw me all right and I could tell from his face, he was shitting himself.' Duke looked from Mostyn to Ganci with a satisfied expression. 'And after that, I came straight back here.'

If he expected a round of applause, he was disappointed. Ganci's own face registered nothing, but when he was with Bernie, he always took his lead from him. Bernie, himself, chewed thoughtfully at his lower lip.

'So he's probably now got your car number,' he said after a long pause.

It was said in a matter of fact tone, but Duke took immediate offence.

'One, he was too scared to notice it and two, it was a car I borrowed from Syd and he wouldn't even tell anyone the time without asking me first.'

'O.K., Les, don't lose your cool, I'm only thinking.'

'The idea was to put the frighteners on him, wasn't it? And that's just the way it was. It was a reminder to him that we're still around and haven't forgotten him. Which was what the frightened little creep was hoping. He thought it was all over now and he could bolt back down his hole out of sight. Today's reminded him that he's not yet off the hook.'

Mostyn nodded in a satisfied way. 'Yeah, I think that's good,' he remarked. His expression suddenly clouded again. 'No chance of your having scared him so much, he'll run to the coppers?'

Duke shook his head vigorously. 'We're O.K. there, he won't say a word to anyone.'

'You say that, but he did once before,' Mostyn said, his tone once more tinged with doubt.

'That was different. He wouldn't have said anything then if that other geezer hadn't spoken up. And the reason he spoke up was because G wasn't very subtle in the way he handled him.' He accompanied the observation with a reproachful look at Ganci who remained impassive. 'Anyway,' Duke went on, 'he hasn't said anything since and now he knows he can't because we can twist his balls off if he does. We've got him really scared, Bernie. Really scared.'

'That's the way I like to have 'em,' Mostyn said with quiet satisfaction.

'What's that word of yours, Bernie?' Duke asked, jumping up to get himself another drink.

'Malleable.'

'That's the one. Malleable. It's just what Pal Weir is. He's as malleable as a ... as a liver sausage.'

Mostyn edged his glass towards Ganci. 'I could use another drink,' he said.

CHAPTER THIRTEEN

Anyone noticing Clare getting out of her car in Leather Place, Wimbledon, that afternoon would probably have taken her for a market researcher. Leather Place residents were used to attractive young girls descending on them and asking earnest questions about the detergents they used, the cereals they ate or a brand of kipper fillets they'd never heard of.

She had given some thought as to what she should wear for her miscellany of visits and decided she couldn't go far wrong with her blue trouser suit and the yellow blouse with its frilled collar and cuffs. She pinned a plain gold and topaz brooch in her lapel. It was one her grandmother had left her and this was the first time she had ever worn it on duty. Finally, before setting off she had breathed on the sapphire of her engagement ring and given it a small rub as if to make it shine better.

Her first call, and the one to which she'd been looking forward to most on a purely personal interest level, had been at the home of Roy King, the pop group manager who lived in Chelsea. The door of his flat had been opened by a girl with blonde hair reaching almost down to her waist. The girl had looked Clare up and down for several seconds before apparently deciding that she was neither a fan nor a competitor for Roy's affections.

'No, he's away in Germany,' she said at length, in answer to Clare's enquiry. 'He'll be back at the weekend. The Fig Leaf are touring there,' she added by way of explanation.

Luckily, Clare was aware that the Fig Leaf was one of the groups which Roy King managed.

'I'll try again later,' she said, turning to go.

'Have fun,' the girl said in a mechanical tone as she closed the door.

Clare couldn't recall ever having met a girl who was quite so incurious. She had asked Clare neither her name nor her business. Clare could somehow picture her mooning about the flat until Roy King returned. She hoped he might get a rather more enthusiastic welcome home than seemed likely. She also hoped, though she couldn't for the life of her think why she should care, that he'd avoid, in future, the sort of carelessness which had resulted in paternity suits and in his appearance in Flo's books of cuttings.

As she set course for Wimbledon, Clare's mind went back to the books of press cuttings. Or rather, to one book in particular.

Just before she left headquarters, she had been looking through the book which had been in current use at the time of Flo's death. Its first cutting was dated four months ago and it was less than a quarter full. Though she had been through it previously, she now observed something which had escaped her notice on earlier examination.

One of the longer cuttings which lay flat appeared to have been originally folded back in the middle. When Clare lifted the bottom edge and let it fall along its fold line it was clear that a smaller cutting had once lain beneath, but had been removed. The larger folded cutting had then been opened out so that it covered the place where the other had been.

Unfortunately, both Nick and Detective Chief Superintendent Peacock had been out at the time and so Clare had kept her discovery to herself. But from time to time as she drove to Chelsea and then onwards to Wimbledon, she puzzled over it.

It wasn't so much the removal of the cutting which was causing her to speculate, as the effort to conceal its removal. Unfortunately, there was no clue whatsoever as to its nature.

It was possible, but by no means certain, that a laborious check of the index cards might disclose which it was, but this was something that would take hours of patient research and must await a later date, provided Peacock or Nick considered it worth the time and effort.

She was still pondering the missing cutting as she walked up and rang the bell of number 18 Leather Place. The door was opened by a woman who looked too old to be the milkman's wife and yet not old enough to be his mother.

'Is Mr Woods in?' Clare asked, giving the woman a friendly smile.

'Which Mr Woods do you mean?'

'Mr Leslie Woods.'

'Yes. Who shall I say wants him?'

'My name's Clare Reynolds, but he doesn't know me.'

The woman stood her ground as though waiting for further explanation of the visit.

'I wanted to see him on a private matter,' Clare added and noticed the woman's suspicion deepen.

'You've not come to serve him with any legal papers or anything like that?' Clare shook her head. 'Are you from the press then?' Again Clare shook her head.

'If I could just see him for a few minutes.'

Leaving Clare standing on the doorstep, the woman disappeared into a room off the back of the hall. The faint murmur of voices reached Clare's ear and then a man emerged and came towards her.

He had thinning sandy hair and an extraordinarily long

neck which was emphasised by the fact he was wearing neither collar nor tie. His expression was amiable, if somewhat wary.

'I believe you was asking for me?'

Clare gave him what she hoped was a reassuring smile as she spoke.

'My name's Clare Reynolds and I'm a police officer . . .'

'You, a policeman?' Woods said, blinking in his surprise. He let out a small groan. 'I suppose that Mrs Johns sent you after all.'

Clare shook her head quickly. 'No, it's nothing to do with that at all. At least, it is, but not in the way you mean. Is there somewhere we could talk inside?'

He nodded. 'We'll go in the front room. Enid doesn't like it being used except when the vicar calls, but I reckon you're as important as the vicar.'

'Enid is your wife?'

He gave Clare a look which conveyed hurt that she could have imagined such a thing. 'My stepmother. My dad married again two years ago. I 'xpect he did the right thing from his point of view.'

They were about to enter the front room when Enid stuck her head round the kitchen door. Disapproval was registered all over her face.

Perching herself on the arm of a chair – she decided it was an appropriately informal stance without erring too far in that direction – Clare said, 'What I've called about, Mr Woods, is to ask whether you received any letters from members of the public about what is alleged to have happened in Mrs Johns' house?'

Woods swallowed hard. 'One or two,' he said, unwillingly.

'Do you still have them?'

'I might have.'

'Were any of them signed?'

'With names, you mean?'

'Yes.'

'No. They was just nasty letters. Lot of nasty people about, I'm afraid. Busybodies and troublemakers, that's what those sort are! No understanding in 'em, no milk of human kindness!'

Clare nodded to indicate that she didn't belong in that class.

'I'm interested to know whether you might have heard from one particular person.'

'Who's that?'

'He's dead now, but he'd cut out press reports of what was supposed to have happened – and we're trying to find out what his interest was.'

'Most of what was in the papers was lies,' Woods said vehemently. 'If I'd been a vindictive man, I'd have sued them in the courts.'

'This man I'm referring to had another press cutting about you, too.'

Woods flushed. 'The horrible minds some people must have!' he said, shaking his head in contemplation of such wicked ways.

'Did any of the letters you received refer to your earlier bit of trouble?' Clare asked in a tone of mild enquiry.

'One did.'

'And you still have it?'

For answer, Woods left the room and Clare heard him go upstairs. When he returned it was to hand her a blue envelope, the writing on which she instantly recognised as Flo's.

It was with a feeling of rising excitement that she extracted the sheet of matching blue paper inside. There was neither address nor date at the top and it began, 'Dear Mr Woods.' Following that, it read:

'I note from my records that this is the second time you have been in trouble for the same thing. I am assuming – and no doubt correctly – that you were "flashing" again and that was why Mrs Johns slapped your face. Anyway twice caught is enough and I very much hope that I shan't see your name in the papers on any future occasion.' It was signed, 'Observant'.

As she finished reading it, Clare glanced up at Woods who was watching her with a rather odd expression.

'Oh, lord,' she thought, 'I hope he's not about to reveal himself to me. If he does, I shall probably slap his face myself. I can scarcely arrest him.'

Quickly she said, 'Was this the only letter you got from this particular source?' He gave an abstracted nod. 'No follow-up phone calls?' He shook his head slowly in the same abstracted manner. 'Do you mind if I take this letter away with me? I'll return it to you later if you want it back.'

He continued staring at, and somehow through, her.

'Thank heaven I can't see inside his head,' Clare reflected as she got up briskly from the arm of the chair and moved purposefully towards the door. She opened it, to the surprise of Enid who had been obviously listening on the other side.

'I'm just off, Mrs Woods,' she said.

'I've brought you your tablet, Leslie,' the woman said, looking in the direction of her stepson. 'You forgot to take it after your dinner.'

Woods seemed to shake himself out of his trance and came out into the hall.

'I'll see this lady to the door,' his stepmother went on. 'You go and give your dad a hand in the garden. He's trying to do too much.' When she had successfully shooed him out of sight, she turned back to Clare who was hovering by the front door. 'He's not in any sort of trouble, is he?'

'None as far as I'm concerned,' Clare replied brightly.

'That last business worried his dad and me stiff and we don't want anything further of that sort. That's why I made the doctor give him tablets. They calm him, you know.'

Clare nodded sympathetically and beat her retreat. As

she drove away from Leather Place, her mind was not, however, on Leslie Woods' problem, but on Flo. What had he thought he was? Some sort of disembodied civic voice administering admonitions to the more frail members of the community? A self-appointed and anonymous keeper of all our consciences?

It took her three-quarters of an hour to manoeuvre her way to Uxbridge. It was the sort of journey she most hated. Built-up area all the way and heavy traffic into the bargain. And when she did reach Uxbridge, it took her further time to locate Fritz Cantor's premises.

Eventually, she parked her car in front of a low brick building which bore a sign saying, 'Fritz Cantor Ltd.'. Behind it was a much larger building, one end of which was blackened and partially destroyed. Several large tarpaulins had been flung across the damaged part of the roof.

'Can you tell me where I'll find Mr Cantor?' she asked a girl who had just emerged from the office block.

'In there,' the girl said, indicating the entrance over which the company name appeared.

'He's in, is he?'

'Yes. You want to see him, do you?'

'Please.'

'Is he expecting you?'

'No.'

'Would you like me to tell him you're here?'

'Thank you.'

'What name shall I give him?'

'Miss Reynolds.'

'What's your firm?'

'I wanted to have a word with him on a private matter.'

'You're not from an insurance company?' the girl asked anxiously.

'No.'

'That's a good thing,' she said in a relieved tone. 'He's having trouble with them at the moment and he can be a bit ... well, you know ... a bit rough-tongued when they call.'

She vanished inside the building. When she returned, she was accompanied by a short, powerfully-built man whom she introduced as Mr Cantor.

'Miss Reynolds, is it?' Cantor enquired, looking Clare up and down.

Clare nodded. 'Is there somewhere I can talk to you privately for a few minutes?'

'What's it all about?'

Clare braced herself for a possible explosion. 'I'm a police officer.'

There was a long pause. Then Cantor said, 'Well, you're a darned sight more attractive than most of the species, but what brings you here?'

'I'm interested to know whether you received any anonymous letters following the fire in your warehouse?'

'Like hell, I did! It was lucky for them they were anonymous or I'd have been doing a few of them up. Bloody cheek, most of them, suggesting I'd burnt it down myself to get the insurance. And I've had nothing but trouble ever since and I'm still waiting for the insurance people to settle.'

'Do you still have the letters?'

'Burnt the bloody things!'

'How many were there?'

'About half a dozen.'

'Do you happen to remember if there was one signed "Observant"?'

'That's right, there was. I remember it because the writer sounded less of a nut-case than the others.'

'You destroyed that one, too?'

'As far as I was concerned, it was another bloody anonymous letter and I chucked it in the fire, but I can more or less remember what was in it. Mr Bloody Observant said that fires were nasty, dangerous things and he hoped my name wouldn't appear in connection with any further ones. Meanwhile he had the neck to inform me that I'd found my way into his records. Whatever that meant!'

'It meant he had filed away the newspaper reports of your fire and opened an index card in your name.'

Cantor's jaw dropped as he listened. 'So you know who he is?' he said, eagerly.

'He's dead. The albums of cuttings were found later.'

'Dead, eh! And you're police! I take it he came to a sticky end then?'

'Yes.'

'Going to tell me who he was?'

'A man called Pewley.'

Cantor frowned. 'I've heard that name.'

'He's the juror who was murdered.'

'Of course! That's where I've seen it. And he was the chap that sent me the letter signed "Observant"?'

'No doubt about it.'

'Well, I never met him and I'm certainly not sorry he's dead. But what was he up to cutting bits out of newspapers and writing to people he didn't know? He must have been a nut of sorts, as well.'

'I agree it was curious behaviour.'

'Curious! There's something creepy about it.'

The girl whom Clare had first seen now reappeared. 'Sorry to interrupt, but you're wanted on the phone, Mr Cantor.'

'Who?'

'It's Mr Smythe,' she said nervously.

'Oh, it is, is it!' he said angrily. Turning to Clare, he added, 'My insurance company. Well, thanks for calling. At least, you've rid my life of one mystery. Drop by again if you're ever in this neck of the woods. You're more decorative than anything in the local copper shop.'

Giving her an abbreviated wave, he shot down the passage to his office.

'Had you finished your business?' the girl asked.

'Yes.'

'I hope you're not cold. I'm sure he didn't mean to be rude not asking you in. Sometimes he forgets where he is. Once he concluded a deal standing out in the rain.'

'Don't worry. Everything went fine.'

Getting back into her car, Clare headed for her final port of call, which was a street off the Shepherd's Bush Road. It was an area full of cheap boarding houses and rooms to let and the house outside which she pulled up had a sign hanging in the front window saying 'vacancy'.

The door was opened by a cheerful faced woman with a huge mound of platinum blonde hair.

Clare reckoned she must either use a gallon of lacquer a day or have pit props within the mound to keep it up.

'Yes, dear?' she said, giving Clare an appraising look. Her tone was studiedly neutral, the result of years of practice of dealing with doorstep callers of every description.

'I'm a police officer. I wonder if I might have a word with you inside?'

'Oh, lord, it's not that girl in trouble again, is it? I wish I'd never set eyes on her. Proper little vixen she turned out to be. And yet to look at her, you'd not have thought she had a wicked thought in her pretty head. And to think I was taken in by her! That's what shook me most of all. Anyway, what's she done this time?'

'I haven't come about her, whoever she is,' Clare said when the woman finally stopped. 'I've come to ask you about a man called Baker.'

The woman, who had led the way into the front room, swung round abruptly.

'Baker? Someone was round here asking questions about him some weeks back. One of your lot, I mean, and I told them then I didn't know what they were on about.'

'Perhaps I can explain, Mrs ...?'

'Pritchard.'

'There was a small piece in a newspaper about two

months ago, Mrs Pritchard, saying that police had come to your address looking for this man Baker.'

'And I told them he wasn't here.'

Clare nodded. 'What I'd like to know is whether any letters came for him here after that?' Mrs Pritchard shook her head vigorously. Dangerously so, in Clare's view, though her mound of hair survived without any apparent sign of an avalanche.

'Were there any telephone calls for him?'

'None. Look, dear, I told the ones that came, I didn't know what had brought them as I'd not seen him for several years. That is, assuming – which they seemed to do – that their Baker was my Mr Arthur. You could have saved yourself a journey if you'd spoken to your other lot.'

'They were from Bristol, I believe. And anyway, my enquiry is quite different. It arises as a result of a murder investigation here in London.'

'The other lot never said anything about murder,' Mrs Pritchard said indignantly.

'It hadn't happened then, that's why.'

'Who's been murdered then?'

'A juror in a case at the Old Bailey.'

'I've read about that,' Mrs Pritchard said in a tone of pride. 'But what's it got to do with Mr Arthur?'

Clare, who had hoped not to have to go into the whole background, sighed as she realised she would have to try and satisfy Mrs Pritchard's curiosity.

When she finished, Mrs Pritchard remarked, 'Well, dear, I've known some funny types in my time, but fancy cutting bits about complete strangers out of newspapers!' She pursed her magenta lips and added primly, 'He doesn't sound a very nice person, if you ask me.' She gave a sudden start. 'Wasn't he the one that was found without any hair?' she asked.

'Yes.'

'I thought I remembered reading that. Well, dear, that

proves it, doesn't it? I've always known there was something funny about men who don't have any hair. Something wrong with their glands, dear! I certainly wouldn't like having one as a lodger. Apart from giving me the creeps, I'd never feel safe at night time. I don't mind men with only one leg or men with beards and I'll even take in coloureds, but I wouldn't have a hairless man here. It's just the way I'm made,' she added, as though this explained everything.

Clare listened patiently to Mrs Pritchard's list of likes and dislikes, which conjured up changing visions of an unseen Mr Pritchard. When she finished, Clare said, 'So my only interest is in whether anyone tried to get in touch with Baker after the last bit of publicity.'

'As I tell you, dear, no one did. From the day he left here four years ago to the day your lot came asking questions, I'd not heard a thing about him.

'How long did he stay with you?'

'Mr Arthur stayed here just over a month. I wish there were more like him. A really nice, polite gentleman he was. Gave me no trouble at all.'

'What did he look like?' Clare asked idly.

'Nice dark hair he had,' Mrs Pritchard said dreamily.

'About how old was he?'

'A proper gentleman's age,' Mrs Pritchard replied, glancing at Clare to see if she understood. Then she added briskly, 'In his early forties, of course.'

'Oh!' Clare said with a smile. 'I hadn't heard that was supposed to be the best age for a gentleman.'

'You'll realise it when you're a bit older, dear.'

'What did you know about your Mr Arthur?'

'He told me he had been a traveller for a firm up in the north, but he had left as he was proposing to go and settle in South Africa and he was spending a month in London fixing things up.'

'And when he left you, it was to go to South Africa?'

'That's right, dear.'

'Did you ever hear from him afterwards?'

'No.'

'I'd have thought he might have sent you a postcard when he got there,' Clare said.

'Well, he didn't, dear.'

'And how were you to deal with his letters after he'd gone?'

'He told me there wouldn't be any.'

'And there weren't?'

'No, there weren't.'

'Did he receive mail while he was here?'

'No.'

'Wasn't that unusual?'

'No, dear, not at all. One of my present lodgers, who is also a very nice gentleman, gets no letters.' She observed Clare's expression and added, 'And I don't ask any questions. Provided my people behave themselves, I don't pry. If they don't behave themselves, I ask them to leave.'

'Do you often have any trouble?'

'That's why I won't take girls any more. They're the ones who cause trouble like the girl I thought you'd come about. The only trouble I have from men is when they try and sneak girls up to their rooms. And I won't have that! It's not that I'm pure-minded, but once you let that sort of thing happen, there's no stopping it. The neighbours gossip, the bedroom doors are forever opening and closing and it wears out the beds, too.' She gave Clare a quizzical look. 'If you take my meaning?'

Clare nodded. 'Well, it's been nice talking to you, Mrs Pritchard. I mustn't keep you any longer.'

'I was on my way out to meet my friend when you came,' Mrs Pritchard said in a demure voice.

'I'm afraid I've made you late. Can I offer you a lift? Do you have far to go?'

'Only to the King's Head on the corner. Mr Gundy won't mind my being late. He always says that the best things in life are worth waiting for.'

'How right he is!' Clare remarked with a laugh.

'Toodleoo,' Mrs Pritchard said chirpily, as they parted on the doorstep.

As she drove back to headquarters, Clare surveyed the information she had gathered and tried to draw some conclusions.

In the first place she doubted whether it would be worth her while making a special trip to try and see Roy King. If he received a communication from 'Observant', it would presumably have been in the same terms as those received by Woods and Cantor, save that, instead of admonitions about indecent exposure and arson, it would have cautioned him against involvement in further paternity suits.

The most curious feature about the letters seemed to be the absence of anything approaching blackmail. There were no demands of money, no threats, nothing, save a stern tut-tut and a warning that the recipient had found his way into the writer's records.

It was extremely doubtful whether their despatch and receipt amounted even to a criminal offence, Clare reflected, though she supposed that splendid old statute of Edward III's reign might be invoked whereby someone can be bound over to keep the peace in respect of conduct of the nature in question. Admittedly it was questionable whether Mr Woods would have been likely to have taken the law into his own hands had he known who'd sent him the letter, but no such doubt existed where Mr Cantor was concerned. He certainly would have given Flo a thumping, if he had the opportunity. So in his case, the sending of the letter did amount to conduct likely to cause a breach of the peace.

This, however, was all academic in the circumstances, but Clare had enjoyed the lectures on law at training school and had always liked to make up her own mind as to what offence, if any, had been committed before the lawyers weighed in with their views.

Anyway, the practical point was that, if the letters didn't amount to extortion, what was their purpose? The only answer seemed to reinforce the view that Flo kept his records purely as a hobby. They were no more than a facet of an extremely odd personality.

Perhaps the sending of the letters met an inner urge to put his otherwise pointless records to some use.

The fact that Baker had apparently not received any communication after the last bit of publicity could be because the cutting itself made it obvious he was no longer at the address in question and there was, therefore, no point in wasting a stamp in sending him a letter there.

It was six o'clock when Clare drove into the Station yard. She hoped that Nick would be in so that she could discuss her findings with him, but she doubted if he'd be there. It was a day on which Peacock had mustered every officer he could and had sent them forth on what he called, trawling operations. At the end, there would be a tremendous pooling and sifting of all the information which had been collected.

The C.I.D. floor was deserted, confirming Clare's expectation, if dashing her hopes. She went to a cupboard and fetched the albums of cuttings. While she waited for Nick's return, she would go through them again, this time with the specific purpose of discovering whether any others had been surreptitiously extracted.

CHAPTER FOURTEEN

After returning from Flo's funeral and the somewhat spiky interlude at the Queen of Hearts, Nick had gone out again in mid-afternoon and, armed with the bizarre photographs which had been taken of Flo in the mortuary, each one showing him in dark glasses and wearing a different wig, made a round of various shops in the vicinity of High Tree Close.

The photograph he produced in the first instance was that of Flo in what Nick regarded as his work-a-day wig.

Though his reception was invariably polite and interested, he couldn't pretend that he was picking up information of great moment.

The man at the paper shop had raised Nick's hopes by saying that he knew Mr Pewley well. Under questioning, however, it became obvious this meant no more than that he saw him most mornings when he called in and bought a paper. It transpired, moreover, that they had seldom discussed anything more important than the weather.

'A nicer gent you couldn't hope to meet,' he had said, basking in the transient glory of knowing someone who had become the victim of murder.

The manager of the small grocery store a few doors away had formed a less charitable view of Flo.

'Looked a little fusspot and acted like one,' he remarked. 'Was always querying prices and bringing items back saying they weren't fresh. Once he even accused me of cheating my customers.'

'Did you know anything about him apart from what you saw of him in your shop?' Nick asked.

'No; nor wanted to. I know the type too well.'

At another shop, the lady at the cash desk acknowledged that she knew him as a customer but, even on that level, it was, she stressed, a very slight acquaintance. She finally ventured the view that he was 'all right'.

At a shop where they sold cigarettes and confectionery, the owner knew him as someone who was a regular purchaser of extra strong mints. It was here Nick also learnt that Flo was a non-smoker, not that that piece of information seemed to carry the enquiry any further.

The man who sold him mints voiced the opinion that

he was a cultured sort of person. But Nick concluded that this impression was largely gained from Flo's ability to string words together rather better than most of his customers.

All in all, Nick reflected, it had been a bit like searching for eagles and catching sparrows.

As soon as opening time arrived, he repaired to The Three Feathers where he could, at least, serve two purposes at the same time.

Apart from a few early regulars who had been waiting for the doors to open and who had retired, pints in hand, each to his own particular corner, the place was empty.

Nick approached the deserted bar and ordered a pint of bitter. The barman was a small, bald-headed man with a friendly expression.

'Not seen you in here before, I think,' he said, handing Nick his drink.

Nick nodded. 'Have one yourself.'

'That's kind of you. Just a small one.' He drew himself a half-pint and raised his glass. 'Cheers.'

'Cheers to you. As a matter of fact I'm after a bit of information.'

'Thought you might be.'

'A man who lives not far from here was murdered recently.'

The barman nodded. 'Mr Pewley, you mean?'

'You knew him?'

'He used to come in here quite often.'

'When did you last see him?'

'A few days before his death.'

Nick felt like someone who turns a tap expecting nothing more than a trickle and is confronted by a steady gush of water without adequate means of catching it. He decided to turn off the tap and start all over again.

'You've not previously been in touch with the police?' he asked in a tone of faint suspicion.

The barman shook his head. Lowering his voice, he

said, 'Didn't think anything I had to say was that important, but chiefly it was the guvnor. He didn't want me to get involved. Thought it'd be bad for business.'

'Generally, it's the reverse.'

The barman made a wry face.

'He's a bit of a funny one, the guvnor. Not too fond of the police.'

'Oh, one of them!' Nick glanced quickly about him.

'It's all right. He's out and won't be back till around nine.'

'Is there likely to be trouble if he finds out you've been talking to me? Incidentally, I'm Detective Sergeant Attwell.'

'No. The fact you came here makes it different. It's not that he's actually obstructive, just non co-operative.' He paused and picked up his glass. 'I'm Ernie, by the way.'

Nick felt that, with these preliminaries completed, he could now engage a further gear.

'How long had you known this Pewley?'

'Over a year. Ever since I've worked here.'

'Used he to come in regularly?'

'As clockwork. Wednesdays and Fridays. Come in about half six, he would, order a Dubonnet – always with ice and a bit of lemon – drink it leisurely like and be gone about half an hour later. He never had a second drink and he never stopped much over thirty minutes.'

'Was he always alone?'

'Never saw him with anyone.'

'Where'd he sit?'

'On a stool at the far end of the bar. He used to perch himself there and just watch everyone. His gaze would flick around like a lizard's tongue. Some people didn't care for it, I know. Occasionally they'd show it, but it never seemed to bother him. He'd still go on sitting there until he'd finished his drink and was ready to go.'

'Used you to talk to him?'

'When I wasn't busy serving, I'd go and have a word with him.'

'What used you to talk about?'

'Any old thing. Except sport. He didn't seem interested in sport, unlike most of them.'

'What sort of person was he?'

'He was all right,' Ernie said indulgently. 'Nothing wrong with him. I quite liked him.'

'What about his appearance?'

'His wig, you mean?' Ernie said with a chuckle.

'You knew he wore one?'

'Not until I read in the paper about him being found without any hair.'

'Then you never saw him in a different wig?'

'As far as I was concerned, it was just ordinary hair, cut a bit stylish. Not that I hold it against him wearing a wig. I've sometimes thought of it myself, but it's too late now. All my friends would laugh if I suddenly appeared with a thatch of hair on top. And just think what'd happen here! They'd probably pelt me with pickled onions when they got a bit merry.'

Nick grinned. He felt himself taking to Ernie more and more. His expression became suddenly serious.

'Wednesday was one of his regular days for coming in, you said?'

'That's right. Except for that last Wednesday when he didn't come.'

'Just what I was going to ask you! Everything points to his having met his death on the Wednesday night, his body being found in Jessamyn Park on Thursday afternoon. You say he didn't come in that Wednesday.'

'Noticed at once and wondered what had happened. Thought maybe he was sick. But it was a particularly busy evening and it slipped my mind until I read about his death in the paper.'

'Had he told you he was a juror at the Old Bailey?'

Ernie nodded. 'He'd mentioned it.'

'What exactly did he say?'

'Just that it was interesting and a nice break from his job.'

'Did he tell you about the case he was trying?'

'No. I asked him, but he said they'd been told not to talk about it outside.'

'Didn't he even mention that it was the Mostyn trial?'

'No, he just said it was one of those dirty book cases. I remember saying in a jokey sort of way that he was lucky to have a nice free read and he did say he'd seen better.'

'And that was all?'

'Yes. He wasn't a great talker at any time. Just used to have his drink and look at everyone, like I said. I always felt he had . . . had secrets in his life. It was nothing he said, just his manner. I didn't really know him any better after a year than I did after the first month.'

'Did the landlord know him?'

Ernie gave a harsh laugh. 'Couldn't stand him. Wasn't his type at all. Wouldn't serve him provided I was here.'

'Why'd he dislike him so much?'

'Regarded him as a kind of snooper, I think.'

Two men came up to the bar and Ernie left Nick to serve them. While he was away, Nick finished his drink and got ready to leave. He seemed to have learnt as much as Ernie could tell him.

When the barman came back, Nick said, 'I must be off now, Ernie. I may be back again. No need to tell your guvnor about my visit unless you want to.'

'I'll see what sort of a mood he's in when he gets back. Probably better to tell him. He acts up if he discovers things he thinks he should have known about.'

'Leave it to you.'

When Nick arrived back at the Station, he immediately sought out Clare who was still assiduously checking through the albums of cuttings.

After they had swapped information, Clare said, 'I've

been right through all the albums again and I'm satisfied there's only this one instance of a cutting having been removed.'

'But you've not found a clue as to which it was?'

'None. It must be one of September this year as the other three on the page relate to July, August and September. And as it was at the bottom of the page, I'm assuming it was September.'

'It could tie in with one of the others on the page.'

'It might, but it's doubtful. If he, or someone else, had extracted one, you'd have expected them also to remove any further one relating to the same person.'

'That's true.'

'In view of what you say about his missing door key, I'm wondering if the murderer didn't return to Flo's flat after killing him and remove the cutting then. If so, it would mean that the cutting related to the murderer – and that the murderer was aware of its existence in Flo's records.'

'First of all, how would he know unless Flo told him and, anyway, what was the particular risk in Flo preserving it? After all, a press cutting is not like an original painting. It has appeared tens of thousands of times over.' He paused. 'But there's an even bigger snag to that theory.'

'What?'

'If it was the murderer who took Flo's door key, why didn't he also take the other ring of keys, without which he couldn't have got to the books of cuttings? They were all locked in a cupboard when we searched the place and there was no sign of it having been broken open.'

'Oh!'

'So that rather scotches your theory, Constable Reynolds,' Nick said, in fairish imitation of Peacock's voice.

'I'm afraid I only caught the end of that,' a voice suddenly said behind them. They both swung round to find Peacock standing just inside the door. Looking at

Nick, he went on, 'Have you got a bad throat?'

'No, sir.'

'Your voice sounded odd,' he remarked with a deadpan expression. 'Anyway, what was Clare's theory and why has it been scotched?'

'You tell Mr Peacock,' Nick said to Clare.

When she had finished, Peacock said, 'And now I'll tell you both something interesting about that. Only one set of fingerprints was found on the cupboard where the albums were kept. Whose do you think they were?' He glanced from Clare to Nick with a sardonic expression.

'I would have said Pewley's,' Nick remarked warily, 'but your question would seem to rule that out.'

'You're right so far.'

Nick's jaw dropped. 'You don't mean ...'

'Yes, I do mean. Yours.'

CHAPTER FIFTEEN

Mrs Brigstock was already settled in her chair and her husband was in the act of switching on the television when the front-door bell rang.

'It's probably Mrs Finch returning my baking tin, but what a time to come. Now, we'll miss the gardening programme.'

Mrs Brigstock made as if to get up from her chair, but her husband waved her back.

'I'll go, dear. I'll tell her you're busy. Don't worry, I'll soon get rid of her.'

But when Mr Brigstock opened the front door with his excuses on the tip of his tongue, it was to discover that it wasn't Mrs Finch standing there with a proffered baking tin, but Vic Fielden.

Mr Brigstock's only reaction was to stare at the visitor with a considerable amount of hostility.

'As you were not at Mr Pewley's funeral this morning,' Fielden said in a self-important tone, 'I thought I should call round and see you this evening.'

'I don't make a practice of attending funerals of people I scarcely know,' Mr Brigstock retorted.

'Yes, you explained that when I spoke to you on the phone, but that's not why I have called.' He looked past Mr Brigstock into the lighted hall. 'Would it be possible for us to talk inside for a few minutes.'

Mr Brigstock hesitated. 'It's not very convenient,' he said, 'but ... well, all right, I suppose so. If it won't take long.'

He led the way into a room he always referred to as the parlour. It was cold and certainly not congenial for a lengthy conversation. Though he closed the door after they had entered, he neither offered his visitor a seat nor made any attempt to sit down himself.

'Have the police been to see you since the trial?' Fielden enquired in a conspiratorial voice.

'No. Why do you ask?' As soon as he had spoken, Mr Brigstock regretted it. He had been determined to evince no interest in the ex-foreman's visit and now he had done just that.

'It's difficult to find out what they are up to,' Fielden observed. 'They've not been to see a single one of us since the day the trial ended.'

'I'm sure they know best how to conduct their enquiries,' Mr Brigstock said, regaining his lofty manner.

'And what's more,' Fielden went on as though Mr Brigstock hadn't spoken, 'we've been offered no protection whatsoever. Here's one of our number brutally murdered and not an official finger lifted to protect us.'

'I wasn't expecting to be protected. I don't consider myself in any danger just because Pewley was murdered.'

'Well, that's where you may be wrong,' Fielden retorted in a tone which caused Mr Brigstock to blink.

'I don't understand you,' Mr Brigstock replied after his momentary loss of composure.

'I told you, didn't I, that I'd arranged a little reunion after the funeral? Well, it provided an opportunity for us to exchange views after paying our last respects to Laurence Pewley. It also became quite clear that Philip Weir is in trouble.'

Fielden paused significantly and Mr Brigstock said, with raised eyebrows, 'Is that all you've called here to tell me?'

'If you'd seen him as we did, you wouldn't adopt that tone.'

'Look, Fielden, as far as I'm concerned, the case is over. We're no longer a jury and we have no responsibilities for each other. Not that we ever did. If Weir is in trouble, all right he's in trouble, but I fail to see how that's any concern of mine. Or of yours. Weir must solve his own problems as best he can. You don't even have any evidence, I gather, that his trouble has anything to do with his having been a juror. It may be anything. A sick wife, difficulties at work, *anything*. My position is that, if the police wish to interview me further, they know where I can be found. Until they do so, I have no desire to become embroiled.' He paused and fixing his visitor with an unfriendly stare, added, 'And I think you would be well advised to take the same attitude.'

He was moving towards the door, when Fielden said, 'But you sat next to him on our jury.'

'What exactly do you mean by that remark?' Mr Brigstock demanded, swinging round and glaring.

'He thought there was something curious about your behaviour. He told me more than once.'

Mr Brigstock appeared to battle silently for words.

'I am not remotely interested in what that foolish young man thought,' he said eventually. 'Moreover, I must warn you, Fielden, that I will not tolerate your going around making insinuations of that sort. Any more of it and you'll be hearing from my solicitor. And now will you kindly go.' He paused. 'And not return.'

Fielden bit his lip. Then with a shrug he said, 'I'm sorry that's your attitude. I felt as a man of the world that I should call on you, despite your hostility towards the rest of us during the trial. A hostility all the more significant in the light of events. Anyway, don't blame me for anything that happens hereafter. At least, I know where my duty lies even if some people don't. And now if I may go ...'

He moved past the speechless Mr Brigstock out into the hall. He had opened the front door when footsteps behind caused him to turn his head.

Mr Brigstock stood there, his face suffused with rage. 'How dare you speak to me like that!' he shouted. 'I'll teach you a lesson, you interfering little busybody! Just you wait!'

CHAPTER SIXTEEN

'You're not in trouble, are you?' Mrs Weir asked in a voice laden with suspicion.

'Of course I'm not,' her son, Philip, replied in a far from happy tone.

'Something's wrong, that's for sure. Look at your plate, you've hardly touched your food.'

'You gave me too much. I told you I wasn't hungry.'

Mrs Weir was a thin, vinegary woman who at no time had exhibited much maternal affection towards her son, even though he was her only child. As a result he had left home and got married at a far too early age. Within three years, there had been a divorce, after which he had lived on his own for a few years until, finally, he had asked if he might take up residence again with his parents. His request had been granted, but without enthusiasm and only after a fair amount of grumbling on the part of his mother, who had made it clear she had no intention of making a slave of herself on his account.

Mr Weir's feelings towards his son had always been those of the bully towards his victim. He now looked up from the evening paper he had been reading during the altercation between his wife and son.

'You haven't fallen in love again, have you?' he asked, with a nasty little smile.

' 'Course I haven't.'

'It's time you did get married again,' Mrs Weir remarked. 'You can't expect me to look after you for the rest of your life. Though next time, I hope you'll pick someone better than Iris. I never did like her from the first moment you brought her back here.'

'Please, mum! Do we need to go through all that again?' Philip asked wearily.

'Anyway, it takes two to make a quarrel,' Mr Weir put in.

'Exactly,' Philip said. 'It wasn't all Iris's fault. We got married too young.'

'Oh, I'm not saying you were blameless,' Mrs Weir retorted quickly. 'Just that I never liked her.' She picked up her son's plate. 'You probably caught a cold at that funeral this morning,' she said in a tone in which sympathy had no place.

Philip nodded and clenched his teeth as they began to chatter.

'What is wrong with you?' his father asked, when Mrs Weir had carried their supper dishes out to the kitchen.

'I keep on telling you, nothing's wrong with me.'

'Bollocks! You've been in a state of jitters for days and this evening you've been worse than ever.

Something's bloody up with you!'

Philip licked his lips nervously.

'Everyone has their problems,' he said, as his father continued staring at him.

'Well, you're certainly old enough to cope with your own. How old are you, incidentally?'

'Twenty-nine.'

'Good lord! To think I've been married to your mother for thirty years. Seems like three hundred at times.'

'I think I'll go up to my room,' Philip said.

When he got there, he sat on the edge of the bed and held his head between his hands. His body became convulsed with uncontrollable shivers and he just stared at the floor waiting for them to pass. At least, there was no one to see him as there had been at lunchtime in the Queen of Hearts.

If he had had any sense, he would have cut that meeting. But then he'd have had to have given Vic some explanation or other and Vic wasn't an easy person to fend off. As it was, he'd thought that, being in company would help restore his nerve after what had happened at the cemetery.

The shock of seeing that man had really shattered him, the more so as he had begun to feel hopeful that the ghastly black cloud which had been suspended immediately over his head had dispersed. And then had come the reminder that it not only hadn't, but that its proportions were more ominous than ever.

The shivering passed and he stared cautiously about his room as though any sudden physical or mental movement would start it off again.

One thing, at least, he could be thankful for. He had not told his parents about the threatening phone call he'd received while he'd been on the jury. And although the newspaper reports on the trial had referred to incidents of intimidation of jurors, they had refrained from mentioning names.

If his parents had by mischance found out, everything would now be that much worse. As it was he could nurse his troubles alone. A trouble shared is a trouble halved might be true in some instances, but not where his parents were concerned, he reflected ruefully.

He got up from the bed and walked across to the window. There was a full moon and clouds were scudding across the sky in aimless competition. Philip stared at the moon wishing that he was on it, if not even further away. Perhaps if he said a prayer, God would wave a wand and by morning everything would be all right. He'd be giving Him almost twelve hours to work His miracle, which was surely long enough. Oh, if only it could happen that way!

It seemed a hundred years since he had sat on that jury and yet certain events were ineradicably etched on his mind. The whole atmosphere of the trial had in retrospect assumed sinister overtones. He felt now that there was no one he could really trust. Mr Brigstock had always been a strangely forbidding character, but there were others he had taken to, especially the bonhomous Vic Fielden. Now, however, he viewed Vic Fielden with suspicion. Indeed, with a considerable amount of suspicion ...

He heard the telephone ring down in the hall. It seemed an age before anyone answered it. Then he heard his mother call out from the bottom of the stairs, her voice strident and cross.

'Philip, it's for you.'

His legs felt as though they were filled with lead as he walked across to his bedroom door.

'Philip!' Her voice became louder. 'Telephone.'

'I'm coming,' he said, as he stepped out on to the landing.

She was still at the bottom of the stairs when he got there.

'Some man wants to speak to you. Wouldn't give his

name.' She gave him a challenging stare.

He nodded as nonchalantly as he could and moved past her to pick up the receiver. She continued to watch him.

'Was that your mum who answered?' enquired a voice which Philip instantly recognised.

'Yes.'

'Is the nosey old biddy still around?'

'Yes.'

'All right, just listen to me and I'll tell you what you've got to do ...'

When the voice finished, Philip said 'yes' once more in answer to the question whether he understood his instructions.

He dropped the receiver back in place and turned to face his mother.

'I shall be going out,' he said stiffly and ran past her back upstairs.

CHAPTER SEVENTEEN

When Nick arrived at headquarters the next morning, there was a message saying that a Mr Fielden had phoned and would Detective Chief Superintendent Peacock please call him back as soon as possible. The message was timed 0830 hours, and it was now ten minutes before 9 o'clock.

Nick knew that Peacock was going straight to the Yard to report to the Deputy Assistant Commissioner in charge of all divisional C.I.D. branches and would not be coming in until mid-morning. He therefore decided to phone the number himself.

From the speed with which the receiver at the other

end was lifted, he deduced that Fielden must have been sitting with his hand resting on it.

'Detective Sergeant Attwell here, Mr Fielden, I understand you phoned about twenty minutes ago.'

'Is Chief Superintendent Peacock there? I'd like to speak to him, if possible.'

'I'm afraid he's out, but can I help you?'

'When will he be back?'

Nick bit his lip. He didn't care for being upstaged in this manner by the likes of Vic Fielden.

'I can't tell you, but if it's anything to do with the case, you can discuss it with me and I'll let Mr Peacock know when he comes back.'

'It's not something I can discuss over the phone, anyway,' Fielden remarked in a tone which caused Nick to place a hand over the mouthpiece and mutter darkly.

'What were you proposing then?'

'I think it would be best if I came and saw the Chief Superintendent personally, but it is rather urgent.'

'Then you'd better come straightaway,' Nick said firmly. 'If Mr Peacock's back, all well and good. If he's not, you can tell me what it's all about.'

After he'd rung off, he went and looked for Clare. He found her in the canteen.

'Didn't you have time for breakfast before you came?' he enquired with a grin.

'I happen to have been at work for a couple of hours already.'

'Good lord, what time did you arrive?'

'Before seven. I wanted to finish my schedule of Flo's cuttings while the place was relatively quiet.'

'And have you?'

'Yes.' She popped a piece of buttered toast into her mouth. 'Why don't you get a cup of coffee and sit down? You're giving me indigestion hovering over me like that.'

'This time next year, it's you who'll be hovering over me while I have breakfast.'

'What makes you think that?'

'It's what dutiful wives do.'

'You've been brainwashed by all those T.V. breakfast food ads. You'll find reality very different.' As Nick continued watching her with an expression of affectionate amusement, she said, 'Do you want me to give you a greasy kiss in the middle of the canteen?' Nick started back. 'I thought that'd galvanise you,' she added cheerfully.

Nick fetched a cup of coffee from the counter, drew up a chair and sat down.

'Have you reached any further conclusion about the cuttings?' he asked.

'I'm more and more inclined to believe they were just a quirky hobby, which is confirmed by my visits yesterday to Woods and Cantor. And I'm convinced blackmail can be ruled out as a motive. There've never been any complaints to that effect and the majority of the cuttings don't lend themselves to blackmailing possibilities.' She paused and lifted her cup slowly to her mouth. She went on in a thoughtful tone, 'I believe that if we followed up further cuttings, the most we'd find is that the persons mentioned in them received the same sort of admonitory letters that Woods and Cantor got. The sort of anonymous letters that most people immediately throw away. And if one or two of the recipients ever did take them to the police, they'd have been told the law had better things to do. After all, the letters which Woods and Cantor received contained neither threats nor abuse.' She put her cup down, carefully straightening it in the saucer. 'Anyway, that's the view I've reached.'

'I've heard of some extraordinary hobbies in my time,' Nick said doubtfully, 'but Flo's wins the all time prize – if it was a hobby.'

'It fits what we know of him,' Clare said. 'A strange, lonely little man with this remarkable memory. Prudish ...'

'I'd have said prurient,' Nick broke in.

'They often go together,' Clare remarked. 'Prurience frequently lurks behind a mask of prudishness. You don't have to be in the police long to discover that.'

'I suppose that is true to an extent,' Nick said in a thoughtful tone.

'Of course it is. But the point is that lonely people frequently feel the need to protect their egos. It may take the form of writing letters to the papers or telephoning the B.B.C., if you're a reasonably normal person, but if you're an oddity anyway, as Flo was by all accounts, then it can take less usual forms. I would guess that Flo got a kick out of capitalising his hobby in the way he did. It fed his ego to write those letters. They made him sound like an omniscient observer, an anonymous big brother, something on those lines.'

'You may be right.'

'I'm sure I am. So you must help me persuade Peacock that I'm right.'

'He mayn't need all that persuading.'

'But if he does?'

'O.K.'

'That means you agree with my theory?'

'Yes,' Nick said slowly, 'I think you've persuaded me.'

Clare looked at him fondly. 'I believe that's why I love you,' she said, in a dreamy tone.

'Because I always come round to your point of view?'

'That'll be the day! No, because you're not a male chauvinist pig. You don't automatically reject views put forward by female subordinates, as some officers still do.'

Nick grinned in a pleased way. 'I'll need time to consider all the implications of that observation.'

At that moment, a voice announced over the loudspeaker system that Detective Sergeant Attwell was wanted at the C.I.D. enquiry office.

'That must be Fielden,' he said. 'He's certainly not wasted any time getting here.'

'Were you expecting him?'

'Yes, that's what I came to tell you, but instead you've been telling me things. See you later, darling.'

Clare watched him go. Her expression was notice to anyone who observed it that becoming Mrs Nicholas Attwell meant much more to her than being Woman Detective Constable Clare Reynolds.

Vic Fielden looked up sharply as Nick entered the C.I.D. interview room.

'Is the Chief Superintendent not back yet?' he asked with a frown.

'No. Now what's on your mind, Mr Fielden?'

Fielden composed his features into an expression of self-importance.

'I've come about a rather delicate matter,' he said, shooting Nick a look as if to check that he was a suitable recipient of confidences to come. 'It concerns a fellow juror, whose behaviour, in my view, merits your attention.' He paused as though to review his words so far. 'I need hardly tell you that I'm the last person to indulge in tittle-tattle and that my visit has been prompted solely by a sense of duty. I am sure your Chief Superintendent who interviewed me at the Old Bailey would agree.'

Nick masked his own feelings about the ex-foreman of the jury and said nothing. Obviously something had happened since the funeral the previous day and he waited to hear what it was.

'I refer,' Fielden went on in the same stilted tone, 'to Mr Brigstock. You have doubtless made your own enquiries about him, but I feel obliged to tell you that I believe him to be involved in some way in what has happened.'

'In the Pewley murder, you mean?'

'I'm not saying he was involved in the actual murder, but I'm sure . . . well, I'm sure he knows something which he has not disclosed.'

'Such as?'

'I've no idea,' Fielden said severely. 'It's not much more than a hunch on my part but it's a very strong one.'

'Based on what?'

'Mr Brigstock was the one juror who remained completely aloof from the rest of us during the trial. At times he was positively rude, particularly to myself.' Fielden's glance challenged Nick to deny the truth of what he was saying, but Nick remained silent and impassive. 'I realise, of course, there's nothing very significant in that by itself, but it's when everything is added together that something sinister emerges. I don't know whether you're aware of the fact, but he sat next to Mr Weir in the jury box?' Nick nodded. 'And Mr Weir was one of the two jurors who was intimidated?' Nick nodded again. 'Mr Weir was frightened of Mr Brigstock, did you know that?'

'No.'

'Well, he was.'

'May I ask how you know?'

'Because he told me.'

'Mr Weir told you that he was frightened of Mr Brigstock?'

'He told me that he wished he didn't have to sit next to him.'

'That's rather different,' Nick broke in.

'I hadn't finished what I was going to say,' Fielden said in a tone of reproof. 'He said he wished he didn't have to sit next to him because he was frightened of him.'

'Did he say why?'

'No, but I got the impression it was something Mr Brigstock had said to him.'

'You've no idea what?'

'No. Philip Weir is a rather nervous fellow and he just shut up, but it was clear to several of us that he was a frightened man. I don't know whether you noticed him at the funeral yesterday?'

'As a matter of fact, I did.'

'Anyone could see he was upset.'

'Yes, I agree about that. And you associate his upset with Mr Brigstock?'

'I do. And it is my belief that if you look hard enough, you'll find a link between Mr Brigstock and Mostyn.'

Nick sat up sharply. 'What's your reason for saying that?'

'I went to see Mr Brigstock last night,' Fielden said in the tone of satisfaction of one who has finally captured the interest of his audience. 'I wanted to confirm my suspicions before coming to see you.'

'And you obviously did?'

'Very much so. Mr Brigstock's reaction to my visit was that of someone with a dark secret to hide. He also displayed psychopathic tendencies.'

'Perhaps you'd better tell me exactly what happened.'

When Vic Fielden completed his recital of events, Nick said, 'Is that everything?'

Fielden bridled. 'I don't know what more you expected! I've told you the truth as it happened.'

'Don't misunderstand me, I only wanted to confirm that you'd left nothing out.'

Fielden shook his head impatiently. 'I hope you're going to follow up what I've told you.'

'You can rest assured about that.'

And that's half the trouble, Nick reflected. We daren't not follow up anything in a case like this. And, after all, whatever personal view he might have formed of Vic Fielden, there was no reason to question his honesty.

He had decided to point an accusing finger at Mr Brigstock. But had he told the truth? And, if not, why not?

At all events, the matter would still have to be followed up. But if, at the end, Mr Brigstock emerged wearing a white sheet, Vic Fielden's own behaviour would come under scrutiny.

Fielden broke in on his thoughts.

'I anticipate that Chief Superintendent Peacock may

well wish to have a word with me himself when he returns. He has my office number and I'll be at home this evening.'

Nick nodded abstractedly. He was wondering what motive Vic Fielden had for acting the amateur sleuth? And what about that evening they'd seen him in Soho? Whatever he'd been up to on that occasion, he had not yet seen fit to mention to the police.

'Qui s'excuse, s'accuse,' Nick reminded himself. He wondered whether it mightn't apply in Fielden's case, though, in suggesting so to Peacock, he'd better avoid any French adage.

After Fielden had departed, he fell into deep thought for a time, then he reached for a sheet of paper and wrote down the names of Pewley, Fielden, Brigstock and Weir in a column on one side. On the opposite side, he wrote Mostyn's name. Then he drew dotted lines from the four names on the left till they converged beside Mostyn's name on the right.

It had seemed rather significant while he was doing it, but after staring at his completed work for half a minute, he crumpled up the piece of paper with an impatient gesture and lobbed it into the waste-paper basket.

CHAPTER EIGHTEEN

By the time Peacock returned, Nick's waste-paper basket was rapidly filling up with balls of crumpled paper and he was reaching the conclusion that the arts of the cerebral detective were not his. All he had done was to write down the names of practically everyone connected with the case, thereafter to ring them in red or transfer them about the page by means of purposeful arrows.

At the end, he had received no blinding flashes of

inspiration and he felt himself no further forward in his attempts to rationalise the conduct of the leading figures. It came as a relief when Peacock summoned him to his office.

'We're going to put the heat on Bernie Mostyn,' Peacock said in a satisfied tone when Nick arrived. 'We've been over every inch of the ground in conference and that's the conclusion we've all reached. We're going to line our sights on Mostyn and keep them on target. The D.A.C. wants us to bring him in for questioning as soon as possible. He says it's vital we make a charge at the earliest moment, otherwise public confidence in the administration of justice will be impaired. I gather Judge Slingsby met the Deputy Commissioner at some function or other the day before yesterday and expressed his private concern that no arrest had yet been made, as he regarded Flo's death as an affront to the whole jury system.' He observed Nick's expression. 'Well, something of that sort, anyway. But the fact is the judge appears to have no doubt that Mostyn's behind the murder.'

'He mayn't have any doubt, sir, but does he have any evidence?'

'That's just what we're going to squeeze out of Mostyn. Evidence.'

There was a silence, then Nick said, 'Fielden's been here this morning, sir.'

'What'd he want?' Peacock enquired without interest.

'He didn't want to talk to me at all, sir, he wanted to see you. He thinks there's something funny up between Brigstock and Weir.'

'Seems to me it was a pretty rum jury altogether. I don't know where they pick 'em these days.' He leaned down and opened the bottom drawer of his desk, fishing around inside for several seconds, while Nick waited. 'You can go on, I'm listening.'

Addressing the top of Peacock's head, Nick continued.

'I think we're bound to go and interview Brigstock,

sir, if only to get a formal denial of Fielden's veiled suggestions,' he said when he reached the end.

'Fielden's trouble is that he doesn't like being out of the limelight. I got that impression the first time I saw him.'

'I agree, sir. On the other hand what he says about Weir squares with my own assessment.'

For a minute or more, Peacock stared out of the window in thought while he drummed on the desk with the fingers of his right hand. Thick, stubby, nicotine-stained fingers, in keeping with a man who had grown up in a rough area of the metropolis, served in one as a young policeman and who had never shirked a punch-up as a measure of last resort.

'There are too many bloody red herrings in this case,' he said disgustedly, still staring out of the window. 'It's time we eliminated some of them. Because' – he switched his gaze back to Nick – 'if we don't, we're going to be in dead trouble even after we've made a charge.' The telephone on his desk gave a buzz and he lifted the receiver. 'He's here now, you mean? ... O.K., Sergeant Attwell will see him ... Have him brought up to the C.I.D.' He gave Nick a crooked smile. 'You can start right away. With Weir.'

For a moment, Nick stared at him stupidly. 'Weir, the juror?'

'That's what I said. You'd better go and see what he wants.'

Nick left the room wearing an extremely puzzled look. First Fielden and now Weir. It was as though some unseen hand was busy at manipulation.

Philip Weir, who was sitting uneasily on the edge of a chair, leapt up with a start as Nick entered. There were beads of perspiration on his forehead and upper lip, which had nothing to do with the temperature of the room and it was apparent he was in an even greater state of nerves than he had been at Flo's funeral.

Nick closed the door behind him and motioned Weir to sit down.

'I understand, Mr Weir, that you've got some information to give?'

Weir's chin trembled violently and Nick thought he was about to burst into tears.

'Yes,' he said. Though it seemed he had difficulty producing even that limited amount of speech. He glanced about him as if contemplating flight.

'Try and relax,' Nick said in a calming tone. 'After all, you've come here of your own free will, so presumably you want to tell us something. Right?'

'Yes.'

Nick waited, but again Weir seemed to have exhausted his vocabulary.

'Something about the murder?' Weir nodded, staring at Nick as though mesmerised by his voice. 'Something you've had on your mind and that's been troubling you?'

'Yes.'

'Well, what is it?'

Weir moistened his lips for the umpteenth time. 'It's something I've been worrying about,' he said in a tense voice. 'I should have told you before, but I was frightened to.' He suddenly braced himself in his chair, clutching the arms as though life's last supports. 'I think I know who murdered Laurence Pewley,' he blurted out. 'It was Mr Brigstock.'

He fixed Nick with an expression of horror. Horror at the implications of his accusation.

'That's a pretty serious allegation to make,' Nick remarked quietly. 'You must obviously have something to back it up?'

'Laurence told me.'

Nick frowned. 'Told you what?'

'That Mr Brigstock had threatened to kill him.'

'When did he tell you that?' Nick asked in a tone of considerable wariness.

'The day before his death, it was.'

'In what circumstances?'

'We took a short walk during the lunch adjournment. He told me then.'

'What exactly did he say?'

'Just that Mr Brigstock had threatened to murder him.'

'Did he say why?'

'No.'

'I presume you asked him?'

'Yes.'

'And?'

'He said it was because of something he'd found out about Mr Brigstock.'

'What?'

'He didn't tell me.'

Nick leaned forward and forced Weir to look at him. 'You do realise what a very serious accusation you're making?'

'Yes.'

'Is it the truth?'

Weir swallowed uncomfortably as though he had a sore throat and nodded.

'You've not answered me. Is what you've just told me the truth?'

'It's the truth.'

'No doubt about it?'

'It's the truth.'

'Because if it's not the truth, you ought to know that you yourself will be liable to prosecution for wasting police time.'

'I've told the truth.'

'All right, as long as we both know where we stand. But I have to ask you this: why didn't you tell us before? You had an opportunity when you were interviewed at the Old Bailey the day after the murder and the best part of a week has gone by since. Why have you waited until now to come forward with such vitally important information?'

'I was frightened.'

'Frightened of what?'

'Of Mr Brigstock. He sat next to me on the jury.'

Nick said nothing for a while. It was almost as if Fielden and Weir must be in some sort of collusion. First, Fielden had come saying that Weir was frightened of Brigstock, to be followed by the alleged victim of fear himself saying the same thing.

'Why were you frightened of him?' he asked.

'It was his manner.'

'You must have a better answer than that!'

'He *did* frighten me.'

'Did he ever threaten you?'

'Not exactly.'

'Either he did or he didn't.'

'No, he didn't actually threaten me.'

'Well, what did he do?'

'I keep on telling you, it was his manner. He had an intimidating way.'

'Give me just one instance?'

'There weren't any instances. It was his whole manner all the time.'

'And you really expect me to believe you went in fear of him?'

'After Laurence had told me he'd been threatened by him and then a day later he was found murdered, yes I was frightened of him.'

'So frightened that you didn't dare tell the police?'

Weir hung his head while his mouth and chin trembled ominously.

Nick let out a small exasperated sigh. The trouble was that coming from Weir, who seemed to be in a permanent state of craven anxiety, the story couldn't be dismissed out of hand, as it might have been had its source been otherwise.

'All right, accepting that you've been too frightened to come forward before, what has induced you to do so now?'

Weir looked up, watery eyes blinking.

'I hoped you'd make an arrest and then I needn't have said anything. It's only because you haven't that I ... I decided I must.'

'Supposing we'd arrested someone other than Brigstock, what would you have done then?'

'I don't know.'

Nick looked at him thoughtfully for a moment.

'Have you ever mentioned your fear of Brigstock to anyone?'

'I think Vic Fielden may have guessed.'

'How?'

'I did once tell him that I wished I wasn't sitting next to Mr Brigstock.'

'Was that all you told him?'

'I think so.'

'You didn't actually say you were frightened of him?'

'I can't remember.'

'Might you have done?'

'I think I might have.'

Nick experienced a deep frustration. He had probed and tested Weir's accusation against Brigstock as well as he could, but without reaching a conclusion. Weir's explanation for not having informed the police previously and for coming forward now was *just* plausible in his case. His fear of Brigstock was also *just* plausible, if you accepted that he believed him to be a murderer at large. His allegation that Flo had told him of a threat to his life by Brigstock was now beyond confirmation. It was significant that this was so in the case of the one firm fact he had advanced.

Nick became aware that Weir was watching him closely. Well, he had one final question to ask him and then he'd go and report to Peacock.

'Did anyone suggest you should come here this morning?'

Weir's mouth opened and shut several times, but no sound came. He licked his lips in an agitated way, but still didn't speak.

'Well?'

'No! No, of course not!'

'Why were you so taken aback by my question?'

'Taken aback? I don't understand.'

'Are you sure you haven't been discussing things with Fielden? Wasn't it he who persuaded you to come here?'

'No. He doesn't know anything about my coming.'

Nick got up. 'O.K., Mr Weir, that's it for the moment. But before you leave, I am going to have all you've told me recorded in statement form. You'll then be asked to sign it. So now's your chance, your last chance, to make any retractions. You understand?' Weir nodded. 'Is there anything you've told me that you're having second thoughts about?' Weir shook his head. 'That means everything you've told me this morning is the truth?'

'Yes.'

'And you fully realise what a serious business it'll be if it turns out otherwise?'

'I've told the truth,' he said, hoarsely.

'So be it.'

When, a few minutes later, Nick knocked on Peacock's door, the voice which bade him enter had a rasp of anger.

'Have you heard what's happened?' Peacock ground out. It was all too apparent that he was in no mood at that moment to listen to anyone else's problems.

'What, sir?'

'Mostyn's disappeared.'

'Any clues where?'

'It is said,' Peacock remarked in a tone of heavy sarcasm, 'that he has gone off for a short break. To have a rest and get away from everything after what he's been through. That is what is said! And to ensure an uninterrupted holiday, he has not left any forwarding address.'

'Looks as though he realised the heat was about to be turned on him, sir.'

Peacock snorted. 'I'll have every person in this country watching out for him before the day's out.'

'Isn't it likely he's already out of the country?'

'I'll have every Frenchman, German and Spaniard doing the same thing. I'll give him holidays!'

CHAPTER NINETEEN

When Nick was eventually able to claim enough of his Detective Chief Superintendent's attention to tell him about Philip Weir's visit, he was listened to in moody silence.

'It's that bloody man Fielden,' Peacock said savagely when Nick had finished. 'He's a meddler. Can't resist stirring things.'

'You think he's put Weir up to this?'

'I don't know what I think about it. I just wish I knew what the hell was going on. I begin to think the whole jury was up to funny tricks.' He paused and frowned. 'I wonder if it's possible that Mostyn had managed to fix a number of them?'

'To ensure his acquittal you mean, sir?'

'For what other reason!'

'If he had, why should he arrange for one of them to be murdered?'

'I know! That's the bugger of it! Nothing fits.' He glared at Nick. 'I said I wanted the red herrings eliminated and now they're multiplying.'

'I thought I'd get in touch with White, sir,' Nick said, ignoring the other's outburst. 'He was the last juror to see Flo alive and I think we ought to find out whether

Flo mentioned his fear of Brigstock to him.'

Peacock nodded. 'And you'd better also check the same thing with the solicitor and those two young lads where he worked. Can't remember their names.'

'Sanderson and Barrow.'

'Right. And if the deceased voiced no fears to any of them, we shall be left wondering why he did so to Weir. And if we conclude that Weir has lied, we shall still be wondering.' He gave an exaggerated sigh. 'Anyway, I'm keeping my sights trained on Mostyn. It's important at times like this not to be thrown off course.' He got up. 'I'm off to Soho. I'll take Inspector Pearce with me. You get on with your enquiries.' Nick was half-way through the door when Peacock said, 'What's Woman Detective Constable Reynolds up to?'

'She's on the final lap of preparing the schedule of cuttings, sir.'

'Good. I'll have a word with her about them when I get back. Tell her, will you?'

Nick nodded. When he reached Clare's room, he found her busy with paste and scissors putting her schedule together.

She looked up as he entered. 'It'll look rather like a patchwork quilt when I've finished,' she said cheerfully.

'The old man wants to see you with it when he returns from a visit to Soho.'

'When'll that be?'

'No idea.'

'So I just hang about and wait?'

''Fraid so. You could do something for me, though.'

'What?' she said in a suspicious tone.

'A button's come off my top-coat.'

'All right, on one condition.'

'What?' It was his turn to sound suspicious.

Clare burst out laughing. 'Now I've got you worried! You really are rather adorable when you wear that look. Anyway, I'll let you off if you kiss me.'

Closing the door behind him with his foot, Nick came across and gave her a quick but fond kiss.

'What was the condition to have been?' he asked afterwards.

'I've no idea,' she said, gaily.

'You mean, it was all a ploy?' he asked.

Clare was still laughing when she said, 'Go and get your coat, if you want me to sew on a button.'

While she switched from her schedule to Nick's coat, he returned to his room to telephone Mr White. Rather to his surprise, seeing that he was calling him at his place of business, White himself answered the phone. It must be that White had given him his own personal office number.

'Would it be possible to see you sometime today, Mr White?' he asked, after a few preliminary pleasantries.

'Yes, I think I can manage that,' White said in a slightly guarded tone.

'I can come to your office or visit you at home this evening, whichever suits you better,' Nick said.

'Hmm.' There was an appreciable pause and then White said, 'Why don't we meet for a sandwich over lunch?'

'All right! Where suits you?'

'There's a quiet little place called The Stewpot not far from Queensway underground station. Suggest we go there.'

'Fine. Shall I pick you up at your office?'

'No ... no, I'll meet you there.'

When Nick returned to Clare's room to retrieve his coat, he was wearing a puzzled frown. Was it his imagination or had Mr White shown a distinct determination to keep their meeting on neutral ground? He gave a shrug. It probably was his imagination, but even if it wasn't, there could be a perfectly innocent explanation. He must guard against indulging in suspicious thoughts about every member of Mostyn's jury.

The Stewpot was certainly quiet and Nick soon saw why. Its prices were way above average and its sandwiches were mere distant reminders of what they purported to be. It appeared to derive its name from the one hot dish on offer, which was stew ladled out of a huge container next door to the coffee machine.

Nick had been waiting for five minutes when Mr White came hurrying in. He walked over to the corner table where Nick had begun his meal.

'Sorry I'm late.'

'Sorry I've started, but I was rather hungry.'

'I'll just get myself something and then I'll join you.' He returned a couple of minutes later with a ham roll and a cup of coffee. 'I knew we'd be able to talk in peace here, it's never crowded.'

'I'm not surprised. This sandwich is the meanest I've had in years.'

'Have you tried your coffee yet?'

'No. And anyway it's tea.'

'The tea's even worse than the coffee, I'm afraid.' Mr White bit into the hunk of bread which enveloped a small piece of ham. 'Any developments since we met at the funeral?' he asked in an interested tone.

'Yes and no. Tell me, how well did you get to know Weir while you were together on the jury?'

'I didn't get to know any of them well. I'm afraid I rather resisted Vic Fielden's collegiate approach.'

'I gathered that, but did you form any impression of Weir?'

'He always struck me as an unusually nervous young man. And he was obviously unnerved by the telephone threat he received. Not that one can blame him for that.'

'Did he ever seem to be afraid of one particular person?'

'Who do you mean?'

'I don't want to put names into your mind.'

'No-o, I can't say I noticed that,' Mr White remarked after a thoughtful pause.

'I think it's now established,' Nick went on, 'that you were the last member of the jury to see Pewley before his death. As you were leaving the Old Bailey, I mean.'

'Oh, yes, yes,' Mr White said, after a second's hesitation. 'I gather that is so.'

His tone struck Nick as that of someone who has just safely manoeuvred a trick bend. Oh lord, I'm growing suspicious of him again, he reflected.

There was a short awkward silence before Nick continued. 'Did he say anything to you about having been threatened?'

'No-o.'

'Did he give you the impression of being a man who'd been recently threatened?'

'Definitely not. What sort of threat was he supposed to have received?'

'A threat to kill him.'

'My last impression of him that evening,' Mr White said in a tone of quiet emphasis, 'was anything but of a man who had any worries on his mind.'

Nick nodded wearily. 'That accords with the impression he gave at his office, too.'

'I think I told you I noticed that big man who was a friend of Mostyn's staring hard at Pewley in court once or twice.'

'Yes, you did. But there's no evidence of Pewley having been upset.'

'I wouldn't know.'

'And nobody else appears to have noticed it.'

'I can assure you it was so.'

'It's not that I disbelieve you. I was just stating a fact. Anyway, it's incredible how much people's observation of the same occurrence can vary. Makes our job all the harder.'

'Do you still regard Mostyn as your chief suspect or

shouldn't I ask that?' Mr White enquired with a small self-deprecating smile.

'The case bristles with suspects,' Nick replied airily.

'Oh, really. I thought it could only be Mostyn.'

'I remember your saying so.' Nick glanced about the still almost empty café. 'Your office is close by, is it?'

'Yes.'

'I don't think I've ever asked you what line of business you're in?'

'It's only a small affair. I'm the agent for one or two South African companies.' He smiled. 'Chief advantage is that I'm virtually my own boss.'

'And you live in Barnes, I seem to remember?'

'Yes.'

'Children?'

'Grown-up.'

'So you and your wife can take life easy these days?'

'My wife left me a good many years ago. I've never re-married.'

'I'm hoping to get married next year. To a girl in the police.'

'Congratulations. She should, at least, be understanding of your unpredictable hours.'

'We're going for a family straightaway.'

'From handcuffs to nappies,' Mr White observed with another small smile.

Perhaps a broken marriage had made him so, Nick reflected, but he was a remarkably self-contained sort of person. Perfectly pleasant and polite but revealing next to nothing about himself. Well, not everyone was a Vic Fielden.

Nick pushed back his chair and got up. Mr White followed suit.

Outside on the pavement, Nick said, 'My car's just down the street, can I drop you at your office?'

Mr White shook his head. 'It's not far and I like to stretch my legs.'

Again Nick had the impression that he was being fended off. Then he gave a shrug. It was Brigstock, not White, who was his immediate source of interest. He had wondered whether to invite White's view of Brigstock, but this, in the circumstances, would have disclosed more than discretion warranted and he had decided against.

Later a visit to the offices of Messrs Tuke and Wirrall confirmed what he expected, namely, that neither Sanderson nor Barrow had received any impression of Flo's life being under threat. Indeed, Barrow repeated that he had seemed particularly pleased with himself on the evening in question.

'I know it's being wise after the event,' Nick remarked, 'but I wish you'd asked him what he meant about bread.'

Barrow nodded ruefully. 'Though if you'd been me at the time, you wouldn't have either,' he said.

Nick emerged from their office to find a lady traffic warden in the act of making out a ticket for his car.

She was a strapping blonde woman whose peak cap looked as if it had accidentally landed on her head.

'Sorry, love,' she said, when Nick told her who he was, 'but once I've begun one, I have to go on. It's the regulations. But the Commissioner will pay, won't he?'

Nick waited impatiently while she continued to make out the ticket which seemed to take her as long as if she were recording his life story.

His next port of call was Mr Brundle's office in King's Cross Road, where he was kept waiting ten minutes before being shown into the solicitor's own room, which smelt strongly of toilet water and wax polish.

'I'm sorry to have kept you waiting,' Mr Brundle said in a somewhat haughty tone, 'but it's so much better if you can phone for an appointment. I might have been out of my office.'

'It was a risk I was prepared to take,' Nick replied. 'In any event, I happened to be passing this way.'

'And what is it I can do for you?'

'Did Mr Pewley ever speak to you about a threat to his life?'

'Good gracious no! I would most certainly have informed you had he done so.'

'Quite. But I'm asking because one of his fellow jurors has suggested he did receive such a threat.'

'I would think it was a ridiculous suggestion,' Mr Brundle said with disdain. 'I'd have been the first to know if there'd been any such threat.'

'Except that you were out of London the few days before Mr Pewley's death.'

Mr Brundle pondered this with his lower lip thrust out, reminding Nick of a spoilt pug dog.

'Anyway, who is supposed to have threatened him and for what reason?' he asked after a pause.

'I don't know for what reason,' Nick replied pointedly.

'I see,' Mr Brundle said with a sniff. 'Well, I'm afraid I can't help you further.' Nick had got up and was about to leave when he added, 'I suppose you haven't yet found the key to my late client's flat?'

'I'm afraid not.'

'I'd have thought that was a significant clue, if ever you wanted one.'

'It may yet prove to be so,' Nick observed cautiously, 'though at the moment it doesn't tie in with anything else.'

'Well, let's hope you make some progress soon,' Mr Brundle said with a small, waspish smile.

CHAPTER TWENTY

As soon as he returned to headquarters, Nick discovered that Peacock, deprived of his principal quarry, had turned his attention on Brigstock.

'I've arranged for him to be picked up and brought

here as soon as he leaves his office,' Peacock said when Nick reported to him. 'We'll put Weir's and Fielden's allegation to him point blank and see what happens. And a police station provides the best sort of atmosphere for that sort of confrontation. There's no doubt about that.'

'Does he know why he's coming, sir?'

'I suppose the very fact that I said I'd like to see him here may have alerted him that something's up. And he's probably connected it with Fielden's visit to him last night.'

'He didn't demur at coming?'

'Demur? People know better than to demur when *I* rattle the handcuffs.'

When some forty minutes later Mr Brigstock was shown into Peacock's office, he had the air of some small, but dangerous, animal taking its first look round the zoo cage which is to be its future home.

His neat moustache was a-bristle, his eyes darted angrily and his whole being radiated an almost palpable tension.

'Sit down, Mr Brigstock,' Peacock said airily, indicating a chair. 'You remember Detective Sergeant Attwell?'

Mr Brigstock flashed Nick a hostile look, but said nothing. He sat down with the air of someone expecting to catch an unmentionable disease from contact with the chair.

'I'll come to the point straight away,' Peacock said briskly. 'It's reached our ears that you threatened to kill Pewley not long before he met his death. What've you got to say about that?'

For a few seconds, Mr Brigstock stared at Peacock with an expression of intense dislike.

'It's a scheming lie,' he said grimly, 'and I know who's responsible.'

'Never mind about who's responsible, I'm interested in finding out what truth there is to it.'

'I've told you it's a scheming lie.'

'Why should Pewley have told someone of such a threat if it wasn't true?'

For a moment, Nick thought that Mr Brigstock was going to pitch forward on to the floor.

'Pewley told someone that?' he said at last in a hoarse voice.

'Yes.'

'Who? Whom did he tell?'

'Don't worry yourself about that. Just tell me why he should have said it, if it wasn't true?'

'What proof have you he said it?'

'Look, Mr Brigstock, I ask the questions and you're supposed to answer them. Want me to repeat it?'

'I don't know why he should have said it,' he ground out, 'except that, from all accounts, he was a nasty little man. All I know is that it isn't true.'

'Did you ever speak to him?'

'No.'

'What? Not a single word ever?'

Mr Brigstock bit his lip as though to restrain, once more, his rising temper.

'I never spoke to him alone.'

'Did you like him?'

'No, I did not. You know that.'

'Why do you say, "from all accounts" he was a nasty little man?'

'From what I've read in the papers since his death.'

'You didn't get on very well with your fellow jurors, did you?'

Mr Brigstock shrugged disdainfully. 'I didn't serve on a jury in order to make friends.'

'You were the odd one out?'

'Is this what Fielden's been telling you?' he asked with quiet venom.

'Don't worry your head about who's been telling us this or that, just answer my questions.'

'I'm not obliged to answer any of your questions,' Mr Brigstock snapped back.

'True, but if you don't, you can't blame me for drawing certain inferences.' Peacock bit thoughtfully at a piece of hard skin on his thumb. 'The position seems to be then,' he went on, 'Pewley tells someone you've threatened to kill him, and shortly afterwards somebody does in fact murder him; another juror goes in fear of you; you make no bones about being at odds with your fellow jurors; and all you can say is that it's lies.' He suddenly fixed Mr Brigstock with a hard stare. 'Not very satisfactory, is it?'

It seemed to Nick as he watched that Mr Brigstock began to shrink. His moustache ceased to bristle, his eyes assumed an anxious, hunted look and even his suit appeared suddenly to hang baggily on him.

'I don't know what I've done to deserve this,' he said. 'It's like a bad dream. I can't really believe it's happening.'

'Well, it is and self-pity isn't going to help you,' Peacock observed, his tone causing even Nick to wince. By God, he could be bloody nasty when he wanted, Nick reflected. 'The only thing that'll help you is a satisfactory explanation as to why – if you're to be believed – so many wicked lies should be told about you.'

Mr Brigstock shook his head as if now too bewildered to utter.

'Of course,' Peacock continued in a tone suddenly full of guile, 'if Pewley was blackmailing you over something, that would cast quite a different light on the whole matter. Is that what was happening?'

He doesn't believe that for a second, Nick thought. The whole interview has become an exercise in opportunism. He's almost brow-beaten and brain-washed him into making a confession.

Meanwhile, Mr Brigstock gazed at Peacock stupidly.

'What could he have blackmailed me about?' he asked, after a pause.

'There you go again, asking me questions. The question I'm asking is, were you being blackmailed?'

'No ... no, I was not. I've never been blackmailed in my life. I've never done anything I could be blackmailed over.'

'I should thing that's unlikely for a start,' Peacock remarked with a note of scorn. 'Have you ever received any anonymous letters signed "Observant"?'

'No-o,' Mr Brigstock replied with a now puzzled expression.

'Sure?'

'Yes, I'm quite sure.'

It was plain to Nick that Peacock was beginning to lose interest in the interview. He had never believed Brigstock to be guilty of the murder and the recent verbal punch-up had apparently satisfied him further.

Confirmation of Nick's assessment came a few seconds later when Peacock said, 'O.K., that's all, Mr Brigstock. We'll let you know if we want to see you again.' He turned to Nick. 'See who's available to drive Mr Brigstock home, Sergeant.' Then getting up, he walked quickly out of the room without giving Mr Brigstock any opportunity of making a riposte.

By the time they reached the yard at the rear of the Station where the car was waiting, Mr Brigstock had gone a long way to regaining his composure.

'I shall, of course, be seeing my solicitors first thing tomorrow morning,' he said with heavy meaning as they walked across to the car. 'Certain people are going to learn that you can't go around slandering someone with impunity.' Nick said nothing and Brigstock went on, 'I also intend taking legal advice about the manner in which I've been treated by the police. It's been quite outrageous. You can tell your Chief Superintendent that I shall most probably bring the whole matter to the attention of my M.P.'

Nick again offered no comment, but opened the car

door for Mr Brigstock to get in. He stepped back as the car drew away with its passenger staring furiously ahead, moustache once more indignantly bristling.

Peacock was back in his office by the time Nick returned.

'He's going to report us to his M.P., sir, and also consult his solicitor,' Nick said as he entered.

'Just what I'd expect of the little twit.'

'You certainly gave him a bit of a trouncing.'

'Short, sharp treatment. That's what was needed and that's what he got.'

'He certainly did!'

'Never did like prigs. And he's a prig if ever I saw one.'

'But not a murderer?'

Peacock made a scornful noise. 'Never did believe that.'

'Then either Weir's made it up or, if not that, Pewley for some reason or other lied to him.'

'Which do you think?'

Nick blinked. 'I'm not sure, sir. I can see arguments both ways.'

'I can't,' Peacock snapped. 'Of course it's Weir who's lying.'

'I wonder what his motive is?'

'That's just what we're going to find out.' Giving the desk a thump with his fist, he added, 'And if you think I was beastly to Brigstock, wait till you see me with Weir!'

CHAPTER TWENTY-ONE

Leaving Peacock to ring round to find out if any trace of Mostyn had yet come to light, Nick went in search of Clare.

He found her still poring over Flo's books of cuttings. 'Had any inspiration?' he enquired, quickly kissing the top of her head.

'I don't know about inspiration, but how's this for deduction? The murderer was not only known to Flo, but actually visited his flat on the night in question.'

Nick shook his head in puzzlement. 'Well, go on, Miss Holmes, how do you work that out?'

'Presumably Flo was murdered in Jessamyn Park near to where his body was found. Agreed?'

'Agreed.'

'We've never found his door key. Correct?'

'Correct.'

'He'd have been most unlikely to have left home without it so there's an inference that the murderer took it from him afterwards.'

'Go on.'

'Why did he do that? It's obvious. In order to return to the flat and wipe it clean of fingerprints; his, the murderer's, fingerprints.'

Nick looked at her admiringly.

'That's a pretty good deduction, darling.'

'It explains why the only fingerprints found were yours.'

'Don't rub that in!' He was thoughtful for several seconds and then said excitedly, 'And it's significant that the area he wanted to wipe clean was round the book case where the cuttings were kept.'

Clare nodded. 'I know. Which brings one to the missing cutting.'

'The murderer went back to remove it.'

She shook her head. 'He couldn't have. The book case was locked and the key to that was found on Flo.'

'Dammit, yes, of course.' He glanced at her hopefully. 'So?'

'If the murderer and the missing cutting are related, the inference must be that the cutting was removed before

Flo's death, probably by Flo himself.'

'How do you work that out?'

'It was done neatly and tidily and, if you remember, the blank space was carefully covered over by a refolding of the cutting above.'

'But if Flo removed the cutting, what did he do with it?'

'Destroyed it perhaps. Or gave it to the murderer.'

'And why did he remove it?'

'If we knew that, we'd probably know what he did with it.'

'Supposing he did destroy it or did give it to the murderer, why did he then have to be killed?'

'Presumably because its removal or destruction wasn't enough to ensure the murderer's security.' Clare frowned slightly. 'This is groping in the dark, but, if Flo wasn't a blackmailer – and we don't believe he was – what was it that made him a menace to someone? Such a menace that the someone was obliged to kill him?'

'You tell me.'

'His phenomenal memory.'

'I don't follow.'

'I'm not sure I do myself. As I say, I'm still groping. But his cuttings were merely the outward and visible sign of his memory. That's right, isn't it?'

'I suppose so.' After another thoughtful pause, Nick went on, 'What you mean is that Flo recognised someone from his cuttings and so became a threat to that person?'

Clare smiled. 'Yes, I think I do mean something like that.'

'The question is who?'

'That was what I was working on when you came in.'

'With what result?'

'I'm not ready to tell you yet. Give me a bit longer to put my thoughts together.'

'You sound like a scientist on the verge of a startling discovery.'

'I am. It's a new recipe for bread.'

'Bread?'

'What Flo was after just before his death. Remember?'

Nick looked at her uncertainly. 'You serious?'

'I'm serious, all right. The question is whether I'm shinning up a gum-tree. Give me a bit longer and I'll let you know.'

'You realise that, as your superior officer, I could order you to tell me what you're up to.'

'Yes; but you won't unless you want to marry a frustrated and embittered wife.'

'At the present rate of things, it's much more likely they'll ask you to stay on and I'll wind up minding the home.'

Clare got up and gave him a quick kiss. 'Don't give yourself ideas!' she said with a cheerful laugh.

Nick rose, too. 'You're not going to do anything reckless, are you?' he asked with a worried expression.

'Like arresting an armed robber single-handed? No, I'm not.'

'No, you're not what?' came a voice from the door.

'Good evening, sir,' Clare said sweetly to Peacock who stood staring at them. 'I was just telling Nick that I had almost completed my analysis of the cuttings.'

'They're another red herring,' Peacock said disgustedly. 'I gather you've not found a single reference to anyone in this case?'

'I'm afraid that's true, sir.'

Peacock turned to Nick. 'I gave her a list of every person I could think of connected with the trial. Defendant's associates, witnesses, jurors, even all the lawyers. Plus a few others, like Brundle. But you've heard what she says, not one of them figure in the Pewley book of records. However, it is at least one more line of enquiry exhausted.'

'There's still the mystery of the missing cutting, sir,' Nick remarked. He looked to Clare for support, but she assumed a stony expression and said nothing.

The faintly embarrassed silence which followed was saved by the telephone ringing. Nick answered it.

'It's for you, sir,' he said, handing the receiver to Peacock.

It was apparent from the light of battle which sprang to his eyes that it was news he welcomed. After a series of brisk monosyllables, ending with, 'I'll be along immediately,' he put the receiver down.

'Ganci's been arrested for possession of an offensive weapon,' he said in a tone of satisfaction. 'They're detaining him at West End Central overnight. We're getting down there right away.'

It took them forty-five minutes to reach the West End, it being the height of the rush hour, and Peacock spent the whole journey staring morosely out of the car window, which left Nick to wonder just what he was expecting to learn from an interview with Big G.

Ganci looked even larger as he was brought into the rather small room which had been put at their disposal. Nevertheless, Nick reckoned that there was very little waste flesh on him. The man had the power of a gorilla.

Peacock shook his head at him in a pitying way.

'What's a chap like you doing carrying an offensive weapon? They're for frightened little runts, not big boys.'

'It wasn't an offensive weapon,' Ganci said stolidly. 'It was a knife and I always carry it.'

'For sharpening pencils, I expect,' Peacock observed with an expansive smile. 'Anyway, that's not my problem. What I want to know is, where's Bernie?'

'He's gone away.'

'I know that. Where?'

'He didn't leave an address.'

'How very inconvenient!' Peacock's tone had a sudden serrated edge. 'But someone knows where he is, don't they?'

Ganci shrugged. 'All I know is, I don't.'

'Has he gone abroad?'

'Maybe.'

'He usually goes to Malta, doesn't he?'

'He has been there, yes.'

'How are you to get in touch with him if something urgent comes up?'

'He said he'd phone every other day.'

'And has he yet?'

'No.'

'When are you expecting a call?'

'It could be tonight.'

'And then he'll learn of your arrest?'

'I don't know.'

'Are you suggesting that Duke or whoever it is who answers the phone won't tell him for fear the news spoils his holiday?'

Ganci shrugged again and stared about the room as though bored by the proceedings.

'If Duke does tell him, do you think he'll come back immediately?'

'Depends on him, doesn't it?'

'Or do you think he'll leave you to sweat it out alone?'

Ganci gave a slight frown, followed by a further dismissive shrug.

'I suppose,' Peacock went on, 'that you expect your present spot of trouble to be all over by this time tomorrow? You think you'll pop up at Bow Street in the morning, plead guilty, pay a paltry fine and be back at the club in time for a drink before lunch. That's what you're expecting, isn't it?' Ganci stared at Peacock with sudden attention. 'Well, don't depend on it, that's all!' Peacock paused as if to give the other time to ponder what he was saying. 'You see, it could be that the police won't be ready to go on with the case tomorrow and will have to ask for a remand. And you know what happens then, don't you?' He paused again as if to let his words sink in. Meanwhile Ganci's expression had become wary.

'The question of bail arises, that's what happens. And should the police decide to oppose bail, I reckon you stand a very good chance of spending the next seven days in Brixton prison.' He glanced at Nick. 'Wouldn't you agree, Sergeant Attwell?'

'One hundred per cent, sir.'

'So that's the lie of the land as I see it,' Peacock said, as one driven to an inescapable conclusion. 'Of course, a great deal can depend on what happens between now and tomorrow morning. If you were suddenly to come over all co-operative, it might make a big difference to our attitude to tomorrow's proceedings. I'm not saying it would, just that it might. It'd probably depend on the degree of co-operation we received.' He gave Ganci a grim little smile. 'One good turn deserves another, as they say.' He threw Nick a sly glance. 'Sergeant Attwell can probably say it in French, if you prefer.'

Ganci's face, never one to reflect much emotion or reveal his thoughts, had nevertheless indicated by a series of slight twitches that Peacock's message had got through. That this was so became clear a few seconds later when he gave utterance.

'What would you do if you knew where he was?'

'Ask him to come back.'

'You wouldn't have him nabbed?'

'I can't answer that. But if we did, he wouldn't have to know how we discovered where he was. If you play straight with us, we'll do the same by you.'

'If he ever found out I'd grassed on him, I'd have to get out before he got me.'

'If you tell us now where we can find Bernie, the offensive weapon charge will be dealt with tomorrow morning, you'll get a fine and be back in circulation before the day's half-way through. And Bernie need never know anything about it.'

'He's bound to find out. There's people at the club who'll tell him.'

'Even if they do, none of them'll know that you've been talking to me. You were picked up by uniformed officers of West End Central for carrying a knife, which is nothing to do with my murder investigation.'

'And if I tell you where he is, you'll see I'm given outers tomorrow?'

'I can't drop the charge, but you won't get more than a fine and, if the case isn't reached and there has to be a remand, the police won't object to bail.'

Ganci let out a long, melancholy sigh, at the end of which he said, 'He's in Spain. Torremolinos.'

'What address?'

'I don't know. Some Spanish bird he met has a flat there.'

'What's her name?'

'I only know her as Maria.'

'Fat lot of help that is!' Peacock's expression suddenly hardened. 'You're not trying to fool me, are you? Because if you are ...'

'I've told you what I know,' Ganci protested.

'Why did Bernie decide to take off for Spain?'

'He wanted to avoid trouble.'

'Meaning he wanted to get me off his tail?'

'I suppose you could put it like that.'

'Was he responsible for that juror's death?'

A shutter seemed to come down on Ganci's expression and he made no reply. Admitting to knowing Bernie's whereabouts was one matter, talking about Flo's murder was clearly something quite different.

'Well, was he?'

'I don't know nothing about the murder,' he said, impassively.

'Do you know about intimidating jurors?'

'I don't know nothing about that either.'

'Did Bernie fix anyone on that jury?'

'I don't know nothing like that.'

'You wouldn't mind seeing Bernie go inside for a spell, would you?'

'I'm not answering any more questions,' he said in a tight voice.

Soon afterwards, Peacock indicated that the interview was over and Ganci was escorted back to his cell.

'Do you think he was telling the truth, sir?' Nick asked when he and Peacock were alone.

'A bit here and a bit there.'

'About Bernie being in Torremolinos?'

'Oh, sure he was truthful about that. He knew if he cheated me over that little deal, he'd have no peace till I settled the score.'

'I was surprised he co-operated at all.'

'He had a reason. We'll ask Inspector Hughes when he comes back. He may know.'

When the officer in question returned, Peacock put the question to him.

Hughes laughed. 'That's perfectly simple! He's just got himself a new bird, a well-upholstered little blonde piece. He's besotted with her. Rumour is he has it off several times a day as well as all night. The thought of seven days in custody was like a glass of milk to an alcoholic. He just couldn't face the prospect.'

Peacock smiled sardonically. 'Well, thanks for letting me know you'd brought him in.'

'Glad you found your journey worthwhile. Have you got enough to charge Mostyn yet?'

'No. But a nice, cosy little chat with him might make all the difference. I wonder if surrender of his passport was a condition of bail? Not that Bernie would find it difficult to get himself fixed up with another. But if he's done that, it'll be a good reason to clap him into custody on his return, anyway.' He moved towards the door. 'Do you think I might have broken Ganci if I'd gone for him harder?'

Inspector Hughes shook his head. 'Not a hope. Ganci's

not a grasser. He only told you what he did because he felt an ache in the fork. And after all, Torremolinos is a big place and a long way off. It wasn't as if he was putting a real finger on Bernie Mostyn.'

Peacock grunted. Later as he and Nick drove back to their headquarters, he said suddenly, 'If Mostyn isn't responsible for Flo's death, why'd he skip?'

CHAPTER TWENTY-TWO

Nick hadn't long arrived at headquarters the next morning when his phone rang and he was told that Sergeant Graves of Muswell Hill wished to speak to him.

In the few seconds before the call was put through, he searched his mind to recall whether he knew the officer.

'Who am I speaking to?' a rather lugubrious voice enquired down the line.

'Detective Sergeant Attwell.'

'Good morning, Sergeant Attwell, I'm Sergeant Graves, Y division, stationed at Muswell Hill. I've just had a report on a missing person which may be of interest to you. Someone by the name of Weir. Philip Weir. Does the name mean anything to you?'

'It certainly does. He was a juror in the Mostyn case.'

'I rather gathered as much,' Sergeant Graves went on in his mournful tone. 'His father has reported him as missing, but it seems it might be a bit more than that. There's a suggestion of suicide.'

'But his body hasn't been found?'

'No, but he left a note which hints at suicide.' There was a sound as though Sergeant Graves was muffling a sneeze. 'Sorry about that! I've got a foul cold. To go on, I'd say it does more than hint, it clearly points that way. The only thing is, and I don't know about you, but I'm always suspicious of suicide notes which are not accompanied by a body. They're so often the first move in a vanishing act.'

'I know. What does his father think?'

'He struck me as a fairly unattractive cuss. A crude, ignorant type. I wasn't too clear what he thought. As far as he was concerned his son had gone missing and had left this note and now he was telling the police and it was all up to them.'

'Was the note definitely in his son's hand-writing?'

'I gathered so, yes.'

'You have it?'

'No, his wife wouldn't let him bring it. Said she'd give it to the police when they called at the house. And that's really why I'm ringing you.'

'O.K., I've got the address, I'll get in the car and go now.'

'I thought you might want to. There didn't seem any point in my getting involved in the missing person angle if it's really part of your investigation.'

'That's fine. Leave it to me.'

'Good. What do you take for a cold?'

'Whisky.'

'Anything cheaper?'

'Bed. Both together is best of all.'

'I can't afford whisky, and bed at my place is about as peaceful as an ants' nest in the day time, what with kids and animals clambering all over you.'

It took Nick just under half an hour to drive to the Weirs. As he pulled up outside the house, he noticed a sharp-faced woman disappear from her sentinel's post at an upstairs window. Before he had time to ring the bell, she opened the front door and made an impatient motion for him to enter.

'It's the neighbours,' she said, by way of explaining

the need to get Nick into the house and out of sight as quickly as possible. 'I'm Mrs Weir. The missing person's my son.'

Nick introduced himself and she gave him a cold, bony, perfunctory handshake.

She led the way into the front room and went across to adjust the net curtains which covered the window before seating herself.

'There's been something up with him for over a week,' she said, without waiting any prompt from Nick. 'He's been nervous and off his food. Mind you, he's never been the robust sort. He's always been one of the withdrawn types, but both Mr Weir and myself could see something was wrong. But he wouldn't admit it. He's always been an obstinate one, too, you see. Weak and obstinate, they often go together. It's been since he was on that jury at the Old Bailey. Didn't say much about it, but it seemed to worry him. I think the strain may have been too much for him and something happened there to upset him. Well, his note makes that clear.'

'I'd like to see the note he left,' Nick broke in quickly when Mrs Weir paused for a second.

'We found it this morning,' she went on without attempting to produce it. 'Or I should say I found it when I went into his room to see why he wasn't getting up. It was just before eight o'clock. You see, Mr Weir and I had been out last night and didn't get back till after midnight. The house was in darkness and we naturally assumed that Philip was asleep in bed. We'd gone out at seven and left him watching television and he'd said he'd be staying in all evening. He was in a worse state than ever yesterday. Didn't go to work after he'd been to the police station.'

'He told you he'd . . .?'

'It's all in the note.'

'Can I see the note *now*, Mrs Weir?'

'I'll fetch it,' she said, without moving. 'Sat around

all day just mooching. Jumped every time the phone rang or the doorbell went. He really got on my nerves and I told him he was getting me down acting the way he was. Of course, he'd had one or two funny phone calls, but not yesterday. Whoever they were didn't call him yesterday, because I made sure I always answered the phone first and I was going to try and find out what was happening.'

'The note, Mrs Weir. It's important I see it before we go any further.'

'I wouldn't let my husband take it to the police station in case he gave it to the wrong person,' she said, getting up and walking to the door. 'It was on his pillow. I saw it as soon as I opened his bedroom door this morning. And, of course, his bed hadn't been slept in.' When she returned half a minute later she was holding a folded sheet of violet notepaper which she handed to Nick. 'He took a sheet of my best paper that I only use for special occasions,' she remarked indignantly.

'Dear Mum and Dad and Whom it may Concern,' Nick read. 'My head has been throbbing ever since I returned from the police station this morning. Just when I hope things were going to get better, they've got suddenly worse. Much worse. Ruthless people have been using me. They just laughed when I told them I couldn't go on and said I had to or they'd tell the police what I'd done. I can't see any way out. Perhaps I could, if my head wasn't throbbing so. But my visit to the police this morning showed me I'm now in it up to my neck. It was awful, like being sucked into a marsh. They had such a hold over me I couldn't get free. This won't mean anything to you, mum and dad, but the police must be told that what I told them about Mr Brigstock wasn't true. None of it. They made me go to the police in order to deflect attention from themselves. They're evil and I hope my death will serve to bring about their punishment.

'Sorry for the trouble I've caused everyone.
Your son, Philip Weir.'

'No doubt about that being his writing?' Nick asked, looking up.

'He wrote it all right.'

'It sounds very much as if he was intending to take his life,' Nick said, slowly. 'Assuming that to be so, how do you think he'd have set about it?'

'Doing himself in, you mean?'

'Yes.'

'At least, he spared us by not doing it in the house,' Mrs Weir remarked stiffly. She frowned. 'It's hard to say. He didn't have a gun, so he wouldn't have shot himself. And he was afraid of heights, so he wouldn't throw himself out of a window. And he was funny about blood, too. Used to make him feel faint.'

'Might he have drowned himself?' Mrs Weir nodded in a thoughtful manner.

'He liked water. He could sit and watch it for hours without moving. It sort of fascinated him.'

'Any particular stretch of water he used to visit?'

'No, just any old water he happened to be near.'

'What's the nearest water here?'

'There's the reservoir. It's about a mile away.'

'If I may use your phone, I'll have an alert put out for him. If we haven't found him by the end of the day, we'll have to think again.'

'Mr Weir thought he might have just disappeared and left that note to put everyone off.'

'It's a possibility to be borne in mind. Particularly, in view of what you say about his recent worries. Suicide is very much the last resort. It's often easier just to vanish and let people think you've done yourself in. Supposing that is what's happened, have you any suggestions where he may be hiding?'

She shook her head. 'Since his marriage broke up, he's been going to Ireland for his holidays. He enjoys walking.

I suppose he might have gone there.' She cast Nick a quick appraising glance. 'Who are these people he refers to in his letter? The people who've made him do things?'

'My guess is that he's referring to people who were involved in the case he was on at the Old Bailey,' Nick said judiciously.

'But how did they get a hold over him?' Her eyes were bright with curiosity.

'I can't answer that.'

She looked away. 'Once when he was at school, an older boy got Philip to steal for him just by bullying him. He's never been a very brave boy. In fact, his father has always said he's a coward.' She paused. 'But then he's a bully, too,' she added bleakly. She rubbed the palms of her hands down over her knees in a smoothing operation and seemed about to go on speaking. Nick waited, but nothing further came.

'Well, I'd better be getting back, Mrs Weir. I'll take the note with me and we'll let you know as soon as we have any information about Philip. I hope it won't be too long.'

She accompanied him to the front door, but stood back when she opened it to let him out. He heard it close behind him almost before he'd taken a step.

As he drove back to the Station, he reviewed in his mind everything touching on Weir's disappearance. In the end he decided he wouldn't be surprised by either of the possibilities. Indeed, whether he'd killed himself or done a carefully prepared bunk didn't greatly affect the issue. What mattered was his confession of being used by Mostyn, in particular with regard to implicating Mr Brigstock.

It remained to be discovered how Mostyn had got a hold over him in the first place.

On his return to the Station he discovered that Peacock had gone to Bow Street, presumably to see what happened to Ganci and decide whether there might be any further opportunity of exploiting his situation.

Next he went to look for Clare only to find that she had also gone out.

'Where's she gone?' he enquired.

'British Museum Newspaper Library at Colindale. Said she might be there all day,' replied the desk sergeant.

'So that's what she's up to,' Nick murmured to himself, without, however, feeling much the wiser. 'At least she can't come to any harm *there*.'

CHAPTER TWENTY-THREE

P.C. Davies stopped his panda car beside the railings which surrounded the reservoir and got out.

The railings were awkward, but not insurmountable to an athletic young officer. Before approaching them, he made sure all the car doors were locked. He still recalled with a blush the occasion he had left his car to chase a youth he recognised as an absconder only to return, not only without his fleeter-of-foot quarry but to find a small boy sitting in the driver's seat trying, mercifully unsuccessfully, to operate the radio.

P.C. Davies arrived with a thud on the further side of the railings and brushed himself down before starting up the steep grass slope which led to the rim of the reservoir.

On reaching the top, he gazed quickly across the huge expanse of placid water which was gently lapping against the side.

There wasn't a person in sight and it was as though he had been abruptly transported on to another planet.

As he let his eyes follow round the edge of the reservoir, he saw about four hundred yards to his right what looked like an irregular black shape partly in and partly out of the water. From this distance, it could be anything. The only certainty was it had no right to be there.

He set off in the direction at a brisk trot. The closer he came, the more clearly defined became the shape, so that when he was still a hundred yards off, he could see that it was a body sprawled face downwards, with its head in the water and its legs on land.

Standing ankle deep in water he lifted the body by placing his hands beneath its arms and pulling it round so that he could rest it face upwards on the path which ran round the perimeter of the reservoir.

It was the first dead body P.C. Davies had seen and he found himself staring at it without feeling. It just looked stupidly helpless like a drunk and with the same unco-ordinated appearance, too. The mouth sagged open and water dribbled out. The eyes were turned up. Plainly nothing he had learnt at training school about artificial respiration would be of any avail.

Leaving the body on the path, he ran back down the grass slope to his car and radioed for help.

By the time the news reached Nick, the scene had shifted to the mortuary. When he arrived there, a pathologist had already begun the autopsy.

It was Philip Weir all right. Moreover, it didn't take the pathologist long to confirm that drowning was the cause of death and that there were no marks or injuries of any description to suggest that death was other than by his own hand.

So, Mostyn's trial had resulted in one juror being murdered and in another killing himself. Somehow the two events must be linked. But how? Everything pointed to Weir having been suborned by Mostyn, but what were the pressures which had been brought to bear on him? And how did Flo's death fit in? And what the hell was Clare up to in the British Museum Newspaper Library which Nick had never even heard of until that morning?

With these questions spinning round his head he drove

back to headquarters in a mood of considerable frustration.

Eliminate the red herrings, Peacock had enjoined him. The trouble was that it was like picking fleas off the coat of a barnyard dog. There always seemed as many left behind.

'Mr Edwin Brundle has been on the phone a couple of times,' the desk sergeant said as Nick passed by on his return. 'Sounded a bit agitated. I've left a message on your table.'

'Thanks, George. I'll call him when I get upstairs.'

Dutifully, Nick did so as soon as he reached his room. While he was waiting to be connected, he wondered morosely what the solicitor wanted this time, the more so as he had come to regard him as a bird of dubious omen.

'Is that you, Sergeant Attwell?' Mr Brundle asked in a tone which immediately put Nick's back up.

'Speaking.'

'I think you'd better come along to my office straight away. I've just made a most important discovery.'

'What discovery?' Nick asked, stonily.

'The vital clue to who murdered Laurence Pewley.'

CHAPTER TWENTY-FOUR

On this occasion Nick was not kept waiting, but was ushered into Mr Brundle's presence as soon as he arrived.

'What's this clue you've unearthed?' he asked at once in a brisk, businesslike tone.

'I don't think there's any question of it,' Mr Brundle remarked. 'It's the clue you've been waiting for. I'd better tell you how I came on it.'

Nick let out a small, impatient sigh. He seemed fated

that day to have to listen to a wealth of preliminary detail before having his curiosity satisfied.

'Having at last obtained a duplicate key to Laurence's flat, I spent yesterday evening there going through his effects and it was while I was doing so that I came upon this clue.' Nick shifted on his chair hoping to spur the solicitor to come to the point. 'You will recall,' Mr Brundle went on in a tone of maddening deliberation, 'that I was out of town at the time of the murder, having gone to stay with my sister in the wilds of Lincolnshire a few days before? You recall my telling you that?' Nick nodded. 'Because it explains why Laurence wrote me this letter.' At this point Mr Brundle picked up an envelope from his desk, only to drop it back immediately. 'My guess is that he was intending to post it the next day, but never had the opportunity. The significant thing about it is that it's dated the day he died. Now let me read it to you.'

'May I read it for myself?'

'Of course, you shall have it in a moment.' Mr Brundle took a folded sheet of paper from the envelope. 'Addressed to me at home, but not stamped,' he observed, holding the envelope up for Nick to see. 'Significant, too, I feel, that he didn't wish to send it to me at the office. And let me say, before you ask, it's definitely in Laurence's handwriting.'

Before Nick's impatient gaze, he unfolded the piece of paper.

'Now listen to this,' he said importantly, starting to read. 'Dear Edwin, Something's happened which I must talk to you about as soon as you're back. Something I must have your advice on, as I'm not sure what I ought to do. I do wish you weren't away at this moment, because I need somebody to confide in and you're the only person I can turn to. It's also something you can advise me about as a lawyer as well as a friend. I expect you're beginning to wonder what it's all about? Well, it's quite simple. I've recognised one of my fellow jurors on the Mostyn case as someone whom the police have been looking for for several years. He's wanted for theft of a large sum he stole when he was a cashier with a firm in Bristol. There's been a warrant for his arrest ever since *and there he is on our jury*. Though, of course, he now goes under a different name. His real name is Baker. I recognised him from a photo which appeared in the paper. The thing is that I let on to him I knew who he was and he was naturally terribly upset. But I said that, as far as I was concerned the past was the past and his secret was safe with me. Since then I've been wondering whether I'm right or whether I have a duty to let the police know about him in some way. I certainly wouldn't wish to go to them directly and I'm not at all sure that I wish to pursue the matter further. Anyway, you now see why I want your advice. As a matter of fact, I've asked him here this evening to show him that I don't intend using my knowledge, as he was so worried about what I might do. But it's several days since I disclosed it to him and I think he's become reassured in the meantime. As you can tell, I've more or less decided that I don't want to do anything about him, but I should still like to discuss it with you, Edwin. I know you'll tell me that I was indiscreet to let him know, but I just couldn't help myself. It's not often that my memory for detail provides me with such an unexpected and astonishing triumph. A real coup, you might say. I've thought it better not to give you his new name in this letter, just in case it goes astray, but I can hardly wait for your return and to having one of our long chats. Yours very sincerely, F. Laurence Pewley.'

Mr Brundle laid the letter on his desk and looked at Nick with a complacent air.

'Not much left for you to do, eh? It's providential I went to the flat last night or it might have lain there undetected for weeks or even months.'

Nick didn't follow the logic of this observation, but forbore to say so.

'Where did you find it?' he asked.

'In the pocket of his grey overcoat, hanging in the hall cupboard. Which is clear evidence that he intended posting it to me once he'd put a stamp on it. He'd probably have gone into the post office on his way to court the next morning.'

Nick held out a hand and Mr Brundle gave him the letter. 'You can have it,' he said graciously, 'I've taken a photostat for my own file.'

As Nick read the letter through to himself, one piece of the puzzle now fell into place. The jokey remark to Sanderson and Barrow about 'bread' obviously referred to the visit Flo was expecting that evening from Baker. A typical piece of Flo humour. It was also plain that he never expected the visit to terminate in his own death, which seemed to show he had misjudged his visitor.

Nick paraded the ten surviving jurors in his mind's eye. One of them was the wanted Baker. Which?

CHAPTER TWENTY-FIVE

Unlike her fiancé, Clare had not only heard of the British Museum Newspaper Library, but had even visited it on a previous occasion. That had been several years ago when she had been reading economics for an extra-mural degree and she had spent the best part of a week researching one facet of her subject in the files of the *Financial Times*. It was one of the few aspects of the course she had enjoyed, even so not sufficiently to sustain her interest.

She had finally told her tutor that she didn't believe

she would ever find the subject compatible and he, with unflattering alacrity, had agreed. Entry into the Metropolitan Police had followed as something of an antidote.

Clare recalled that on the previous occasion she had been armed with a reader's ticket. This time her warrant card would have to serve to get her in. It was a potent document and she didn't doubt that, coupled if necessary with some feminine charm, it would operate as an open sesame.

She was right, it did.

As a result of careful homework on Flo's book of cuttings, she was satisfied that her quest was not as hopeless as the proverbial search for a needle in a haystack. The item she sought was no less than the missing cutting and she reckoned her chances of finding it as about even.

In the first place, it had almost certainly come from a newspaper between the beginning of July and the end of September, a spread of approximately ninety days.

Next, she had observed that over ninety per cent of the cuttings came from *The Sun*, the *Daily Telegraph* or the *Evening Standard*, so far as the daily papers were concerned and the *News of the World* as a Sunday paper. These were the four papers he seemed to read regularly. Clare regarded it as a blessing that cost prevented him buying others. At least, she presumed that was the reason, for otherwise his strange hobby would surely have inclined him to buy every paper on the stall.

These were her thoughts as she sat waiting for the first instalment of her requisition to be fetched.

The attendant, who had studied the list, had shaken his head in gloomy disbelief.

'All this lot, miss?' he had enquired.

'I'm afraid so. But I shan't keep them long.'

'Once I've brought them, you can keep 'em all day,' he said, grumpily. 'It's the fetching 'em what takes the time.'

'I realise that and I'm sorry there are so many.'

'Well, you'd better sit down. It'll take me about fifteen minutes to get the first lot up here.' He paused. 'Did I hear someone say you're in the police, miss?'

'Yes.'

'My son's in the police. He's an inspector.'

'In the Met?'

'No, in the Lancashire force. He married a girl from Preston and moved up there to live fifteen years ago.' He gave Clare a quick up and down glance. 'You're not an inspector, are you?'

Clare laughed. 'Good gracious, no. I'm only a constable, but I'm engaged to a sergeant.'

'My son passed all his promotion exams first time and he's now an inspector,' the attendant observed in a tone of dreamy pride.

'You must be proud of him.'

'Oh, yes, I am that,' he said reflectively. 'Well, I'd better go and make a start on this lot or you'll be here all day.' He glanced at the list in his hand again. 'You most likely will be anyhow.'

When he returned in just about the fifteen minutes he had forecast, he was pushing a trolley. 'These are all your *Telegraphs* for July,' he announced, dumping a stack of papers in front of Clare. 'You can be getting on with those while I fetch the next lot.'

Clare thanked him and set to work. By the time she had gone through the first copy, she realised she would have to improve her speed, or, let alone not finishing that day, she'd risk being late for her wedding.

It was unlikely that what she was looking for would appear on any of the sports pages or the leader page or the foreign news pages and she could therefore safely skip over these.

The result was that by the time the attendant arrived back with another batch, she was over half-way through the first lot, having established a rhythm which allowed her, on an average, just under a minute per copy.

And so the morning passed and one o'clock came with her mind numb and her eyes feeling as though they had never gazed at anything but newsprint.

She pushed the last paper from her and stood up. The awful thing was she couldn't be confident that she hadn't already missed the very item she was looking for. The fact that she didn't know what it was didn't make it easier for her.

Seeking out the attendant, she told him that she was proposing to take a half-hour break. Two cups of black coffee and an egg sandwich later, she was back at her seat.

For another hour she worked her way through a further pile without any glimmer of hope. There was nothing which struck an evocative chord in her mind. Nothing, that is, until she reached the *News of the World* of 26th August.

Her brain reeling from the concentrated monotony of her task, she was about to turn a page when some reflex caused her to focus her attention on an item in the right hand column. It was headed 'Where are they now?' Beneath the heading appeared the photographs of three men for whose arrest, it was said, the police held warrants. Beneath each photograph appeared the subject's name and a brief description of what he was alleged to have done. There followed a general piece on how wanted persons often evaded arrest by adopting fresh identities and a completely new life style so that their disappearance left a mystery which frequently accompanied them to the grave. Their old friends and acquaintances never did find out what happened to them and their new ones never had an inkling of their previous lives.

Having read the whole article, Clare returned her attention to the bit that interested her most.

It was a photograph of Gordon Arthur Baker who had absconded with £12,000 of his firm's money five years previously, who had been traced to an address in Shepherd's Bush, but who had thereafter vanished as completely as a curl of smoke in a breeze.

It wasn't just the familiarity of the name that held Clare's attention, nor the face of the man which was anyway unknown to her, but the fact that the photograph and the text with it were, as far as she could judge, the exact size of the cutting which had been removed from Flo's album.

Clutching the paper as though it might suddenly fly from her grasp, she went and looked for her friend, the attendant.

'Found what you were looking for?' he enquired, seeing the paper in her hand.

She nodded. 'Would I be allowed to take it away?'

He looked at her aghast. 'Not even the Queen could do that! But I tell you what, miss, seeing that it's police business I'll wangle you a photostat copy. I'm not meant to, mind you, but as long as you don't let on, I'll do it. Show me the bit you want copied.'

When, half an hour later, Clare got into her car to drive back to headquarters, she was feeling quietly triumphant. She was certain that she had in her possession a key piece to the puzzle of Flo's death, for she, too, had deduced that Gordon Arthur Baker was synonymous with the dead man's hitherto inexplicable interest in bread on the night of his murder.

CHAPTER TWENTY-SIX

Before leaving headquarters to go and see Mr Brundle, Nick had phoned Peacock at Bow Street Magistrates' Court to give him the news of Philip Weir's death.

'Aah!' Peacock had said in a heavily reflective tone. 'I'm glad you called me.'

He had then sought out Inspector Hughes and said he would like to see Ganci before he came up in court.

'You can almost hear the steam coming off him this morning,' Hughes said with a chuckle. 'One night of abstinence and he's ready to jump out of his pants at the first sight of a female form.' He lowered his tone. 'I'm not sure that even matron's safe,' he added, as a plump, motherly figure in a blue overall passed behind them.

Ganci looked up with an expression of almost comical anxiety when his cell door was unlocked to reveal Peacock with Hughes standing just behind him.

''Fraid something's come up,' Peacock said with a deprecating shrug. He gazed dispassionately at Ganci before adding, 'I hope we can still work our deal, but it rather depends on you.'

'What are you telling me, guvnor?' Ganci asked in a hoarse tone. 'You can't let me down now. I've done all I can to help you.'

'Not quite all. I want a bit more help. As I say, something new has come up since we had our talk last night.'

Ganci licked his lips and slowly shook his head as though unable to comprehend such an undeserved twist of fate.

'What is it you want?' he enquired harshly.

'I'm glad you asked as I'm sure everything can still turn out all right with a bit of co-operation. You remember that one of the jurors for Bernie was called Weir?'

Ganci's expression became suddenly wary. 'I didn't know what their names were.'

Peacock looked at him pityingly. 'That's not a very good start.'

'What makes you think I knew their names?'

'Because Bernie had a list of their names and addresses in his office at the club. That's why.'

Ganci looked away to glare at the floor. 'What about this Weir?'

'That's more like it,' Peacock said affably. 'He's dead. Drowned himself.'

Ganci's gaze met Peacock's. 'What am I expected to do? Send a wreath?'

'No. Nor play funnies with me.' A pause. Then, 'He left a note. In it, he makes it clear that Bernie had a hold over him. I want to know about that.'

'It was Duke, not me.'

'Go on.'

'What's going to happen if I talk?'

'Our deal goes through.'

'But who'll know?'

'I won't shop you to Bernie, if that's what's worrying you. That's a promise. Nobody'll know we've had this further chat. I won't come into court. I won't even leave by the main entrance, so no one'll know I've been here this morning.'

'I'm not signing any statement.'

'I'm not asking you to.'

'It was Bernie's idea we leant on a couple of jurors,' Ganci said with an air of sudden decision. 'He picked the two. Weir was one of them. Duke phoned him and told him to mind his step like. After Weir had reported it, I was all for laying off, but Bernie said anyone could see he was as frightened as a rabbit and we could twist his tail again, but this time much harder so that he'd be too scared to say anything again. And that's what happened. Duke used to phone him and sort of persuade him to see it Bernie's way. He got him so that he'd have jumped off the Post Office Tower if he'd been told. And then after the murder, Bernie said we must get him to tell the police something which would throw them off Bernie's scent. Duke got him along to the club one evening and

Bernie really put the frighteners on him. Told him that unless he did what Bernie wanted, he'd end up in an early grave.'

'Which he's done anyway.'

'I didn't have anything to do with that part. It was Bernie and Les Duke.'

'Why did Bernie want us off his scent so badly?'

'Who wouldn't? Nobody wants the law sitting on his tail, does he?'

'Not when he's committed murder, no!'

'You're wrong about that, guvnor, Bernie didn't murder that juror.'

'Do you know that for sure?'

'It stands to reason. It wouldn't have made sense for him to do it. All Bernie wanted was to be acquitted. That juror's murder was just aggro for him.'

It was at this point that Peacock was summoned to take another phone call. Also from Nick and this time reporting on his interview with Mr Brundle. When he returned to the cell, it was to find that Ganci was now in court.

It was with a thoughtful air that he slipped out of a side door and made a surreptitious departure.

Nick, who had been waiting impatiently for his return, was standing outside the door by the time Peacock reached his office.

Peacock threw his coat down on one chair and his hat on another in what seemed to be a gesture of defiance at life in general.

'Let's see this letter then,' he said, putting out a hand.

Nick handed it to him and watched while he read it with an air of someone determinedly chewing his way through a particularly stale bun.

'Why didn't we find this?' he asked when he reached the end.

Nick blushed. 'Because we didn't make a full enough search, sir. Brundle found it in the pocket of an overcoat hanging in a cupboard. We didn't go through all his clothes.'

'That really is the reason, is it?'

'Yes, sir.' Nick sounded puzzled.

'I just wondered whether there was any possibility of it having been planted, that's all,' Peacock remarked.

'None at all I'd say, sir. Anyway, Brundle swears it's in Flo's handwriting.'

'Hmm. So who is it?'

'I think Clare may be able to help us on that, sir.'

'Where is she?' Peacock demanded, glancing about the room as though she was hiding behind a piece of furniture.

'She went to the British Museum Newspaper Library and hasn't returned yet.'

'What was she doing there?'

Nick shook his head. 'She was on to something, but didn't want to say what until she made some checks.'

'Do you mean,' Peacock asked in an incredulous tone, 'that she refused to tell you what she's up to?'

'I'm afraid so.'

'That doesn't augur well for your marriage, does it?'

Nick grinned. 'I'll have more authority over her then.'

Peacock gave him a pitying glance.

'Anyway, the position is that Woman Detective Constable Reynolds is out detecting and we don't know when she'll be back. But we do believe she may be able to help us on her return. Is that the measure of the situation?'

Nick nodded. He always felt like kicking his Detective Chief Superintendent when he adopted his ponderous manner.

'And why do we think she may be able to assist us as a result of her visit to the British Museum Newspaper Library?' Peacock went on in the same tone.

'I think she was on to something to do with the missing cutting, sir.'

'Oh!'

It seemed to Nick that because Peacock's own favoured line of enquiry had patently run into the ground, he was going to be extremely grudging in his embrace of anyone else's.

Peacock picked up Flo's letter off his desk and read it through again with a moody expression.

'Why the hell couldn't he have said whom he was talking about?' he asked in a peevish tone. 'Why couldn't he have said who Baker is?' He looked up aggressively at Nick. 'Who do you think he is?'

'You asked me that just now, sir, and my answer's the same.'

'You didn't answer my question last time. You just said we'd better wait for Clare's return. You must have formed some theory of your own?'

Before Nick had time to speak, there was a knock on the door and Clare appeared. She looked flushed with excitement and her eyes had an unmistakable sparkle in them.

'Ah!' Peacock exclaimed. 'The very person we've been waiting for.' He stretched out a foot and nimbly removed his hat from the chair. 'Sit down and tell us what you've found out.'

For answer, Clare opened her briefcase and pulled out a couple of photostats.

'I'm pretty sure, sir,' she said, 'that this is a copy of the missing cutting. It's a photograph of Gordon Arthur Baker. I wonder if you or Nick recognise him?'

It was half a minute before either of them spoke. Then jumping up from his chair, Peacock said, 'You're a very clever girl,' and kissed her warmly on the cheek. 'And now you may do the same,' he said to Nick.

It was shortly before seven that evening that the car bearing Peacock and Nick pulled up outside a house in a terraced row.

It was the home of the man they sought. The man who had murdered Flo.

Exhibiting a seam of ruthless determination that moments of dramatic action can call forth from seasoned police officers, even those of Peacock's age, he reached the door of the house and pressed the bell. Nick stood just behind him, observing the muscular hunch of his shoulders as he waited tensely for the door to open.

Footsteps could be heard approaching on the far side and then the door opened to reveal an astonished-looking Vic Fielden.

CHAPTER TWENTY-SEVEN

As Peacock stared at the open-mouthed Fielden his expression changed to one of slow-burning detestation. Detestation of an unwanted and all too intrusive element in his life. Then pushing him aside with a vigorous sweep of his arm, he charged into the house.

'Where are you, Baker?' he shouted, as he burst into the first room he came to. It was empty.

Nick who had followed him in had the impression of being caught in the wake of a rampaging rhinoceros, as his Detective Chief Superintendent thrust his way through each door in turn, though without any sight of his quarry.

The last door he came to was locked.

'Are you in there, Baker?' Peacock called out, furiously rattling the handle. 'It's the police. Come out! Baker, do you hear me?'

There was no reply and he bent down to peer through the keyhole.

'See anything, sir?'

'No, but I can feel something. A bloody great draught.

It's the bathroom. Come on, put your shoulder to the door.'

The flimsy lock stood little chance against the combined thrust of Nick's and Peacock's shoulders and in seconds they had hurtled through the doorway to the accompaniment of a loud splintering of wood.

The bathroom window was wide open and Peacock dashed across and leaned out.

'He would have to live on the ground floor,' he muttered angrily. 'Nip out and see if there's any sign of him.'

Nick clambered through the window on to a small iron veranda and dropped three feet on to the soft earth. Heavy footprints beside his own told him all he needed to know and a quick look around sufficed to confirm that there was no one hiding.

At the far end of the tiny patch of garden was a dilapidated wooden fence with a footpath on the farther side which, he could see, led into a parallel road.

He gave the fence a frustrated kick and a piece of rotten wood fell away. The whole place might have been designed for an easy get-away.

Returning to the house, he climbed back through the bathroom window. He found Peacock in the living-room with an anxious-looking Vic Fielden.

'No sign of him, I'm afraid, sir.'

'Didn't think there would be. It seems he was looking out of the window when we drove up. He quickly said he wanted to go to the lavatory and he asked Mr Fielden to answer the door when the bell rang.' He glanced round the room until his eye alighted on the telephone. 'With any luck we'll pick him up quite quickly.' He lifted the receiver and began dialling. 'Meanwhile, have a good look round the place.' As Nick moved to the door, he added, 'And don't overlook any overcoat pockets!'

The man whose real name was Gordon Arthur Baker made a final adjustment to the wig he had put on and grimaced. He wished that this particular item of his changed appearance hadn't been necessary. He not only disliked it for itself, but the more so because it reminded him of the cause of his present trouble. Not that he had known Pewley wore a wig until it became dislodged in his death struggle. For some reason he had never quite analysed, he had stuffed it in his pocket and later burnt it. He had since wondered whether it was really necessary to have killed Pewley, but the risks involved in allowing him to live had seemed too great, even after the dead man had given him the tell-tale cutting which bore his photograph.

He had always hoped that his true identity was lost for ever and, with each year that passed, this hope had become strengthened. Nevertheless, he had been aware that the chopper might fall at any moment. Indeed, his whole life these past five years had been conditioned by that ever present possibility and he had alerted his senses so that the chances of being taken by surprise were, at least, diminished.

For several days he had felt that the police were getting closer to him. Some instinct had warned him to bring his arrangements for flight to a state of full preparedness.

Turning away from the mirror he removed his normal dentures and replaced them with a set of uneven, yellowing teeth, which, together with the wig, gave him a completely altered appearance.

Next, he went across to a wall safe and removed a black leather briefcase. Unlocking it with a key from his pocket, he satisfied himself that the wads of £5 notes inside were intact. Seeing that he had only checked it two days previously, it was an unnecessary precaution, but when you are about to discard your present self for ever, you tend to check and re-check the details.

A quick look through the drawers of his desk and he would be ready to go. In one of them, lying on top of a lot of papers, was the document that had summoned him for jury service. He gazed at it with dispassion. Plainly, if he had tried to excuse his attendance, which had been his first thought, he would not be in his present predicament. But on reading the instructions which accompanied the summons, he had reached the conclusion that he might draw more attention to himself by trying to get out of serving than by obediently turning up at the Old Bailey.

It was always easy to be wise with hindsight, but, at the time, he had no reason to believe that jury service would entail any greater menace than going to the cinema or riding on a bus. How was he to know that it was going to bring him into contact with someone with a freak memory like Laurence Pewley?

He closed the last desk drawer, picked up a pair of heavy rimmed spectacles which were the final item of his disguise and put them on, making sure he didn't disturb his wig.

Glancing at his watch he saw that the time was twenty minutes to eight. He had not found an immediate taxi on fleeing the flat and had wasted precious time looking for one. Thereafter, however, everything had gone smoothly and he had been less than ten minutes attending to his current preparations.

He picked up the black briefcase and moved swiftly and silently to the door. A final look around the room and he switched off the light.

'It's time to be going, Mr Mason,' he murmured to himself with a small, wry smile as he unlocked the door to let himself out.

For a second he stood rooted. Then Nick stepped forward from the shadows.

'I'd scarcely have recognised you, Mr White,' he said.

CHAPTER TWENTY-EIGHT

Clare recalled the time at school when the girl who sat next to her in class neglected to invite her to her birthday party. She had experienced the same sense of slight when Nick and Peacock dashed off, leaving her at the Station. It wasn't so much that she had expected otherwise, but more the manner of their departure which left her with a feeling of affront. It was almost as if they had patted her on the head and told her to stay behind and knit a pair of socks.

Nevertheless, she determined to await their return, as her curiosity couldn't be satisfied until she knew the result of their visit to White's home.

She heard a car swing into the yard at the rear of the Station and hurried over to the window to look out.

She saw there were three people in the back. The near-side door opened and Nick got out, followed by Baker alias White, followed by Peacock. Nick took White by the elbow and steered him firmly towards the entrance with Peacock on his other side.

When they had disappeared inside the building, Clare turned and stood indecisively in the middle of the room. Well, at least she had the satisfaction of knowing that her contribution to the investigation had been worthwhile.

She was still standing there in thought when Nick dashed into the room.

'We've brought him in,' he said excitedly, 'and it's largely thanks to you, darling.' He kissed her warmly, which quickly melted whatever reservations she was harbouring.

'Yes, I saw you arrive. Do tell me what happened.'

Nick did so. When he reached the point where he and Peacock had driven with breakneck speed to White's office in Bayswater, he said, 'I thought there was a chance we'd find him there and it paid off. He'd never been keen for me to see exactly where his office was, so after I met him for lunch that day, I made a small recce afterwards, having got the address from the telephone people. It was lucky I did as it meant we didn't waste any time getting there this evening. After the way he fled the flat, it seemed likely he'd made for some stepping-off place where the necessities for further flight were waiting.'

When Nick finished, Clare said, 'It must have almost given him heart failure when he opened the door and saw you.'

'I don't know about *him*, but it almost did me. For one awful moment after I'd accosted him, I wondered if it really was him.'

'What was Fielden doing at his flat?'

'Just busybodying again, as far as I could gather. I can see him arranging reunions years ahead for what's left of his jury. He'll probably design them a tie with a motif of jurors impaled on the sword of justice.'

Clare smiled. 'Well, one has to admit, they are a unique, if diminishing, band.'

'I must dash back downstairs,' Nick said, 'or the old man'll be shouting for me.'

He gave her another kiss and flew from the room, leaving her staring after him with a resigned expression.

Two minutes later, however, he was back.

'Detective Chief Superintendent Peacock presents his compliments to Woman Detective Constable Reynolds and insists that she attends the interviewing and charging of the prisoner.'